FRIENDS *of* LIBERTY

FRIENDS *of* LIBERTY

by

BEATRICE GORMLEY

Eerdmans Books for Young Readers
Grand Rapids, Michigan • Cambridge, U.K.

Text © 2013 Beatrice Gormley

Published 2013 by Eerdmans Books for Young Readers,
an imprint of Wm. B. Eerdmans Publishing Co.
2140 Oak Industrial Dr. NE, Grand Rapids, Michigan 49505
P.O. Box 163, Cambridge CB3 9PU U.K.

www.eerdmans.com/youngreaders

13 14 15 16 17 18   8 7 6 5 4 3 2 1

Library of Congress Cataloging-in-Publication Data

Gormley, Beatrice.
Friends of liberty / by Beatrice Gormley.
pages cm
Summary: Sally Gifford, a Patriot shoemaker's daughter, tries
to maintain her close friendship with Kitty Lawton, the
daughter of a Loyalist official, as pre-Revolutionary War
tensions in 1773 Boston increase and push them apart.
ISBN 978-0-8028-5418-6 (alk. paper)
[1. Best friends — Fiction. 2. Friendship — Fiction. 3. Loyalty — Fiction.
4. Social classes — Fiction. 5. Family life — Massachusetts — Fiction.
6. Boston (Mass) — History — Colonial period, ca. 1600-1775 — Fiction.
7. United States — History — Revolution, 1775-1783 — Fiction.]
I. Title.
PZ7.G6696Fri 2013
[Fic] — dc23
2012048444

To Lisa,
for her years of friendship

CONTENTS

1

SISTERS AT HEART

One August afternoon in the seaport of Boston, the incoming tide was flowing past Fort William's brass cannon at the entrance to the harbor. The water lifted the British warships inside the harbor and swelled under the crafts crowding the wharfs, from the largest merchant ship to the smallest rowboat.

From the waterfront, cobbled streets ran uphill to the Common, Boston's public green. Just downhill from the Common, on Marlborough Street, a brick mansion stood out as the grandest house in the neighborhood.

In a row of shops on Winter Street, between Marlborough Street and the Common, a sign with a buckled shoe singled out one shop as a shoemaker's. A small frame house, invisible from the street, was attached to the back of the shop.

The kitchen door opened, and a girl in a gray dress

and white neckerchief stepped out. In contrast to her plain clothes, her eyes were bright blue, and her cheeks were even pinker than usual with excitement. Closing the door, Sally Gifford felt for the treasure in her pocket. Yes, the mother-of-pearl brooch was still there, tucked into its little pouch. Her cousin Ethan had made her the special pouch from scraps of glove leather.

Sally stepped nimbly over rows of onions and cabbages in the yard between the house and the cowshed. Reaching the alley, she brushed through a gap in the hedge around Mr. Lawton's grounds. She had no time to waste.

Felicity Gifford, Sally's stepmother, had told her to come home when the clock on Christ Church struck five. "I won't forget the time, ma'am," Sally promised. "There's a chiming clock in the Lawtons' parlor." Of course that was the wrong thing to say to Mrs. Gifford, who gave a scornful sniff. She already thought Edmund Lawton spent too much money on showy luxuries.

The church bells had already struck four o'clock. Sally ran past the Lawtons' stable and through the orchard, between beds of lavender, to the back door. She knocked, but then she lifted the latch and entered without waiting. The housekeeper, Mrs. Knowlton, and the other servants were used to Sally's coming and going.

A trill of notes from Kitty Lawton's spinet at the front of the house told Sally where to find her friend. She hurried down the hall to the open parlor door. "Kitty?"

The music stopped, and the other girl jumped up from

the bench. "So you did escape!" Kitty's eyes sparkled.

Sally laughed. "Yes — I escaped from the Wicked Step-mother!"

Seizing Sally's hands, Kitty pulled her into the room. "Did you bring your — ?"

Sally nodded. Her heartbeat sped up at the mention of what she and Kitty planned. Last time they met, Kitty had suggested exchanging remembrances of their mothers, both of whom had died in the smallpox epidemic of 1764. "That will make us even more than friends."

Sally had hardly dared to believe that Kitty meant what she said. Kitty Lawton, with her blond curls, graceful manners, and mischievous sense of fun, wanted to be more than friends with *her*! If they trusted each other with a token from their dead mothers, they would be like family. "Like sisters at heart," whispered Sally.

Now the girls sat down together on the bench with their backs to the spinet, Kitty's fine muslin skirt brushing Sally's gray homespun. Kitty pulled an object from her pocket: a little white box, no bigger than a walnut shell, with an enameled rose on the lid. She handed it to Sally, and Sally handed her the pouch with the brooch. Kitty said, "You go first."

Sally opened the hinged lid, thinking that such a pretty box could be a memento in itself. The box was lined with black silk. And nestled inside —

Sally gasped. Gleaming in the mellow light from the parlor window was a gold ring. "Oh, Kitty! This must be worth — " More than the Giffords' whole house with all their belongings, she guessed.

"Try it on," Kitty urged. Her eyes shone.

Sally picked up the ring, but then she noticed a lock of blond hair threaded through the gold. It was a mourning ring, a ring specially made to remember a loved one who had died. This must be Kitty's mourning ring for her mother. "Oh, no." Sally hastily put it back in the box. "I couldn't possibly — what would your father say?"

"Papa won't know, will he, if you keep it in your pocket?" A ripple of giggles escaped from Kitty. "It's *my* ring. I may give it to you if I wish."

Sally knew that wasn't true. The father was the head of the household. A daughter had to obey him, at least until she married and left his house. Sally was sure Mr. Lawton wouldn't approve of Kitty giving her mourning ring away — especially to the shoemaker's daughter.

Closing the lid, Sally held the box out to her friend. But Kitty clasped her hands in her lap. "Sally! Don't you *want* to be my sister at heart?" Her voice trembled.

Kitty was hurt. Sally couldn't stand that. "Of course I want to, only — don't cry, Kitty. I *will* keep the ring for now. See, I'm putting it in my pocket." She gave Kitty the empty box.

Kitty hugged her, sniffling. Sally felt lightheaded, as if the two of them were floating. Being sisters at heart was riskier than she'd expected.

Pulling a handkerchief from her ruffled sleeve, Kitty dabbed her eyes and smiled. "Good! Now it's my turn."

She loosened the drawstrings of the little leather pouch and shook the heart-shaped brooch out into her palm. The pin, with its inlay shimmering blue, green, and pink, had always been a treasure to Sally. But she was afraid it would look like a cheap trinket to Kitty, compared with the gold ring.

Kitty didn't seem to mind the difference, though. "This belonged to your mama?" She placed her hand with the brooch over her heart, as if imagining it on a lady's scarf. She kissed the brooch and dropped it into her pocket, handing the pouch back to Sally. The girls hugged again.

It was only last winter that Sally had seen Kitty for the first time. The Lawtons had just moved into the brick mansion on Marlborough Street, around the corner from the shoemaker's shop. Sally had often walked past the mansion's front door, framed by half-columns, with a polished brass knocker shaped like a scallop shell. Kitty's father was a wealthy merchant; many of the ships sailing into Boston harbor carried cargo from around the world for Edmund Lawton.

Although Sally had never expected to step inside the Lawtons' grand house, she wasn't surprised when the Lawtons' carriage pulled up in front of Mr. Gifford's shop. William Gifford was a master of his craft, making shoes to order for the wealthiest people in Boston. On that winter morning when Kitty, escorted by the Lawtons' housekeeper, arrived to have her feet measured for shoes, Sally was sweeping the shop. Sally had watched Kitty step onto a piece of paper in her stocking feet for Mr. Gifford to trace.

Sally couldn't help staring. Not only were the Lawton girl's stockings knit from glossy silk thread — but they had never been darned. Sally's own wool stockings were mended over and over, until the toes and heels were entirely made up of darning thread.

That day, Kitty had seemed like a princess to Sally. Now the princess was her sister at heart.

A warm breeze wafted through the open parlor window in puffs, like breathing. Then Sally became aware of rough music in the distance: a drum beating, shrill fifes, and men's voices shouting a song.

Kitty frowned. "The Sons of Liberty. They're gathering at their tree."

"Ethan wants to join them," said Sally apologetically. Her cousin Ethan, who lived with them, was also her father's apprentice. Lately she'd seen him with Harry Cole, an older apprentice and the leader of a gang.

"Who cares about Ethan?" said Kitty. "You're so different from him, I can't believe you're from the same family! You're naturally refined . . . he's uncouth . . ."

Sally smiled uncomfortably, feeling that she ought to defend her cousin. "He made the pouch for my brooch," she said. But her voice trailed off as Kitty waved away any more talk of Ethan.

Turning around on the bench, Kitty pointed to the music rack. "Look — I have new music. Papa ordered it from London for me. Let's play, and then we won't mind that noise." She began to pick out the upper part of the piece, striking the keys with long, sure fingers.

Sally joined with the accompaniment, keeping up as best she could. Kitty had been teaching her to play the spinet for several weeks now, and she seemed delighted at Sally's progress. Still, Sally couldn't read music as well as her friend. She stumbled over a series of chords, lost her place, and stopped. "If only I had more time to practice . . ."

"Never mind," said Kitty. "Let's play something we know by heart."

As they played the familiar piece, Sally relaxed, floating on delicate ripples of music. She could hardly believe that six months ago, she'd never set foot in a room like the Lawtons' parlor. A fireplace made of marble! French wallpaper, with draped figures lounging among pillars and cypress trees! A clock for the use of just one family! It was as if time in this room was a different time, outside ordinary life.

A portrait above an upholstered chaise showed a young woman with upswept blond hair, wearing a low-cut green embroidered gown. Resting one slim hand on a lacquered Chinese table, she gazed admiringly at a man standing on the other side of the table. The man, wearing a blue silk suit with silver buttons, looked out of the gilt frame with a satisfied smile. He was Kitty's father, Edmund Lawton. The woman, Kitty had told Sally, was her mother as a new bride.

In the pauses between playing, Kitty chatted. "I'm so glad you came this afternoon! I was about to die from *ennui* — that's French for boredom. Not even James is around." James was Kitty's younger brother, twelve years old like Sally. "He went to the docks to record the height of the tide, or some such *fascinating* scientific tidbit."

Sally laughed. James's scientific pursuits were a joke between them. Sally herself had seen James with his face comically blackened from a scientific explosion; Kitty had told her of the time a frog jumped out of James's pocket at the dinner table when Governor Hutchinson was visiting.

James was a strange boy. Although he was civil enough to Sally when he was paying attention, sometimes he walked right past her without noticing. Kitty said her brother often did the same to her. "Lost in his scientific thoughts!" Sally gathered that Mr. Lawton wished James would show as much interest in the business of importing and exporting. Edmund Lawton had named his business "Lawton & Son," expecting that James would begin working with his father as soon as he finished school.

Kitty put the sheets of new music back on the rack and began to teach Sally the accompaniment. "You'll learn this in no time," she promised. Sally glowed with the encouragement; it was true that every time they played, her fingers seemed to know their way over the keys better and better.

Just as Sally thought she was getting comfortable with her part, there was a *crack-crack-crack* outside that sounded like gunshots. Kitty screamed, and both girls jumped off the bench.

Sally's fright faded quickly. "That's only firecrackers. They're setting them off at the Liberty Tree."

"Of course, the *Sons of Liberty*," said Kitty in a sarcastic tone. She sighed. "If only Colonel Leslie would bring his troops into the town! Then the ruffians wouldn't dare to disturb the peace."

Sally wondered if Kitty was right. A few years ago, when the British soldiers had been quartered right in Boston and drilled on the Common, the Sons of Liberty had made plenty of trouble. For one thing, they'd tarred and feathered a man who dared to inform on smugglers.

The girls left the spinet and leaned out the window to peer down Marlborough Street. The Liberty Tree, a huge elm, spread its branches at the corner of Essex Street, a short walk away. Sally glimpsed some men and boys at the edge of the rally, shouting the Liberty Song over the fifes and drums. Sally had heard Ethan singing that song so often that she knew the chorus: "In Freedom we're born and in Freedom we'll live."

Kitty cocked her head. "Listen — are they playing bagpipes, too?"

Sally had also heard the odd sound, but it wasn't at the rally. "It's coming from the other direction." Bagpipes gave her the shivers; their moaning sounded almost like a creature in pain to her.

Kitty leaned out farther to peer up the street, then screamed again. "James!"

At the same moment, Sally realized that the moans were not bagpipe music.

2

The Smell of Tar

Kitty dashed for the front door. Sally ran after her, out to the street. Kitty's brother stumbled over the cobblestones toward them, one hand on the side of his neck.

"What happened, James?" cried Kitty. She reached out to him, but he drew back. She insisted, "Let me see!"

"Tar," he groaned.

Now that they were close to James, Sally could smell warm tar. Sticky black blobs spattered his left sleeve and neckband. When Kitty pried his hand from his neck, the skin was an angry red with puffed, shiny blisters. "Poor James!" she wailed.

Sally winced. She was ashamed that only a few minutes ago, they'd been making fun of James.

As Kitty hustled her brother into the house, calling for Mrs. Knowlton, the clock of Christ Church struck five. It was time for Sally to go home, but she followed Kitty inside. She couldn't leave when Kitty was so worried about James.

Mrs. Knowlton, a neat, plump woman with a keen glance, met them at the door. "Dear heavens, what now?" She steered James into the library. "Take off your jacket — there. Let me see, James. Dear heavens!" The housekeeper turned to Sally. "Run to the kitchen. Fetch clean cloths and the burn ointment."

Sally ran to the kitchen, where the maid found the cloths and Mrs. Knowlton's herbal ointment. When she returned, the housekeeper and Kitty had James stretched out on a chaise with the neck of his shirt open.

Kitty stroked James's hair and tried again to find out what had happened. James groaned, "Tide . . . Apprentices."

"Leave him alone, dear. Can't you see it hurts his neck to talk?" Mrs. Knowlton pulled up a chair and began to spread ointment on the blisters. "Go fetch the brandy and a spoon."

Sally followed Kitty into the dining room. "I'd better go home," she said in a small voice.

"No, please stay!" Kitty, lifting a cut-glass decanter from the sideboard, cast her a look of distress.

So Sally stayed, and the girls watched Mrs. Knowlton dose James with a spoonful of brandy. Kitty took Sally's hand. "Poor James!" she sighed.

Ordinarily, Sally would have been happy to stand in the Lawtons' library, gazing around at its bookshelf-lined walls. In its way, it was as wonderful a room as the parlor. A ladder, for reaching the books near the ceiling, leaned against one wall. A globe of the world tilted on a mahogany stand, and a microscope and a prism — a three-sided bar of clear glass — rested on the side table. The other day, while Sally was waiting for Kitty, James had showed her how the prism could split a beam of white light into the colors of the rainbow.

As the housekeeper bandaged James's neck, Sally shifted her feet. She was touched that Kitty wanted her to stay. Imagine, Kitty was comforted by having her, Sally, by her side! But every minute that Sally stayed at the Lawtons' would make it that much harder for her to slip into the kitchen at home and take up her chores quietly.

When the hands of the clock on the carved bracket shelf reached a quarter past five, Sally squeezed Kitty's hand. "I *have* to go." She hurried out before Kitty could make another plea.

Running down the hall, Sally felt her pocket flap against her legs with a new weight. The ring! She'd meant to give it back before she went home. Well, she'd have to give it back tomorrow.

In the Giffords' kitchen, her stepmother greeted her with a hand on one hip and Baby Lucy on the other. "What time is it, Sarah Gifford?"

Sally hung her head. She knew she was in trouble when her stepmother called her by her full given name, "Sarah." "It's after five o'clock, ma'am, but the reason — "

"The church clock just struck a quarter past." As Felicity Gifford talked, she tried to keep Lucy's grubby little fingers from tugging at her bodice. "You see, I know exactly what time it is, even without a fine *chiming clock* in my *parlor*. Did Mr. Lawton forget to wind his clock?"

"No, ma'am." Sally started to explain about James getting burned with tar.

But Mrs. Gifford cut her off again. "Serves him right, idling around the harbor with other good-for-nothing boys. In any case, what business was it of yours?"

Sally put her hand over her pocket, feeling the ring through her skirt. It was her business, because James was Kitty's brother, and she and Kitty were sisters at heart now. But she only answered, "No business, ma'am."

"And what *was* your business at five o'clock?"

"To set the table for supper, and mind the baby, and cut the bread . . ." Sally glanced sideways at the kitchen table, already set with a spoon at each place and a platter of bread in the middle. "I'm sorry, ma'am." She held out her arms for Baby Lucy.

Lucy began to whine, but Sally swiftly lifted the baby into her high chair at the table, belted her in with a dish towel, and set a row of bread crumbs in front of her. Lucy tried to keep on whining as she picked up the first crumb and put it in her mouth, and Sally laughed at her. "No more fussing!" The baby smiled, showing her six teeth, and popped another crumb into her mouth.

Felicity Gifford had turned back to the stone fireplace, which took up one wall of the kitchen. She muttered into the chowder pot, "I suppose it was too much to expect, that the younger sister would be as industrious and obedient as the older."

Sally pretended not to hear, but she made a face at Lucy behind her stepmother's back. Mrs. Gifford seemed to think Sally's older sister, Hannah, was the perfect daughter. At Hannah's wedding last year, when Hannah left the family for Tom Greene's farm in Concord, Felicity Gifford had shed tears.

The door from the shop opened, and William Gifford appeared. He was a short man, but wiry, with a pleasant boyish look. His thinning brown hair was pulled back and tied at the nape of his neck. Behind him was Sally's five-year-old half brother, Josiah. The boy wore a leather shoemaker's apron like his father's, only one quarter the size.

Hanging his apron on a peg, Mr. Gifford asked, "Is Ethan not home?"

Sally shook her head. Smarting from her stepmother's scolding, she hadn't wondered why Ethan wasn't home yet. Ethan Downs, her fourteen-year-old cousin, was always hungry. In the two years he'd lived with them as Mr. Gifford's apprentice, he'd never been late for a meal.

"No," Felicity answered her husband. "Did you not let him go to the Liberty Tree?"

"*Mmph.*" Mr. Gifford bent over the washstand in the corner, splashing his face. As he toweled his hands and face he added, "Aye, I let him leave the shop early to go to the rally at the Liberty Tree. But he knows what time we eat supper."

"We eat supper at half past five," Josiah piped up. He

14

climbed on a stool to take his turn at the washstand. "That's when the small hand of the King's Chapel clock points to the five and the great hand points to the six."

This brought a smile to William Gifford's face. "You learned something new today, did you, little man?" Pulling out his chair at the head of the table, he leaned toward Baby Lucy and chucked her under the chin, making her squirm and giggle. Meanwhile, Felicity ladled chowder into bowls, and Sally set a bowl at each place.

Mr. Gifford's smile faded as he looked at Ethan's empty chair. "If the lad misses grace, he'll miss his supper, too." Sally felt sorry for Ethan, but at the same time she was glad she wasn't the only one to come home late.

Just as they all bowed their heads for the blessing, the latch clattered. The door burst open, and Ethan slid into his place across from Sally with a muttered apology.

Mr. Gifford went ahead and said the blessing, but then he turned a stern face on his nephew. "You apprentices seem to be getting the wrong idea about liberty. 'Liberty' means we in the colonies have the same rights as other Englishmen. 'Liberty' does not mean that lads of fourteen years may do whatever they like. Tomorrow you will make up the time you took off from your work."

"Yes, sir," said Ethan. His tone was respectful, but he seemed to be thinking about something else.

Felicity Gifford put in, "Some *girls* are getting wrong ideas about 'liberty,' too."

Sally kept her eyes on her chowder and said nothing.

But she thought it was unfair for her stepmother to bring up Sally's tardiness to Father. Mrs. Gifford had already scolded her for coming home late.

Mr. Gifford only gave another *"Mmph"* and began spooning up his chowder. He didn't really want to hear every little thing Sally did wrong. Of course, if he knew that his daughter had given Kitty his dead wife's brooch, and taken a costly gold ring in return . . .

Sally's stomach fluttered, as if she'd stepped into a hole without looking. She wished it were tomorrow already, so that she could return the ring. Kitty must be having second thoughts, too, even though she was bolder than Sally.

But their families need never find out, Sally assured herself, if the girls gave back the tokens at the first chance. Meanwhile, she ought to be as daring as Kitty.

Dipping bread into her butter-flecked chowder, Sally cast Ethan a sympathetic glance. He answered her with the slightest crinkling of his eyes, not enough of a smile to annoy his uncle.

After William Gifford had finished his second bowlful, he sat back in his chair and sighed. "Was there a good crowd at the Liberty Tree?" he asked Ethan.

"Yes, sir." Ethan looked relieved that his uncle was no longer angry with him. "They said it was hundreds! Some of us apprentices climbed up in the tree so we could see."

"I suppose Ebenezer Mackintosh was in charge of events," Mr. Gifford went on. Mr. Mackintosh, also a shoemaker, was a leader in the Sons of Liberty. He didn't do fine work like William Gifford, and his shop was in Boston's South End, a less expensive district than the neighborhood near the Common.

"Mr. Mackintosh was there — I saw him telling Harry Cole something — but he didn't speak to the crowd. Colonel Hancock spoke, and then Mr. Adams." Ethan pronounced the last name reverently.

"Mr. Samuel Adams," said Mr. Gifford, not so reverently. "That man reminds me of a sheepdog. He nips and he barks, and he won't rest until he has all of Boston trotting in his direction."

Sally's father voted with the Whig party, and he was friendly, at least, to the men in the Sons of Liberty, a secret branch of the Whigs. The Sons of Liberty met at the Bunch of Grapes tavern, where Mr. Gifford went for his after-supper pint of ale. Sally often heard her father humming the Liberty Song as he cut and stitched shoe leather.

However, William Gifford didn't make a show of his Whig loyalties in front of well-to-do Tory customers like Mr. Lawton. And he wouldn't leave his workshop for a Liberty rally.

"I thought I heard musket fire from down at the Liberty Tree," Mrs. Gifford put in. She blew on a spoonful of chowder to cool it, then held it to Baby Lucy's mouth.

"No, ma'am — that was only firecrackers," said Ethan. "Colonel Hancock's men were giving them out." John Hancock was the richest merchant in Boston, as well as the head of the Boston militia.

As Ethan reached toward Sally for another slice of bread, she noticed black spots on his homespun shirtsleeve. "You came too close to the firecrackers," she remarked. But even as she spoke, she caught a whiff of a distinctive smell. Not gunpowder — tar.

"Do I see tar on your sleeve?" asked Mrs. Gifford, frowning at Ethan's shirt. She gave a tired sigh. "Tar won't come out in the wash. And only Monday I scrubbed and bleached that shirt."

Casting a sideways glance at his sleeve, Ethan looked troubled, then carefully blank. "Yes, ma'am," he said. "I'm sorry, ma'am." He stopped talking and wiped the inside of his chowder bowl with the bread.

Sally was troubled, too. Why did Ethan look uneasy? Not because he had to wear a dirty shirt — she was sure of that. Maybe he'd left the Liberty rally and gone down to the harbor, where sailors melted copper boilers of tar to caulk their boats.

Kitty's brother, James Lawton, had gone down to the harbor this afternoon, and he'd come home with an ugly burn from hot tar. "Apprentices," he'd said. Had some apprentices ganged up on James because he was a Tory boy, the son of a rich man who hobnobbed with the hated customs commissioners and Governor Hutchinson? It seemed very likely.

Sally knew that these days Ethan hung around a gang led by Harry Cole, a butcher's apprentice. She wouldn't be surprised if it had been Harry's boys who'd burned James badly enough to raise blisters. But if Ethan had been one of them . . . The idea made Sally feel sick.

3

CLEVER GIRL, SALLY

That night Sally wore her pocket, a cloth pouch tied around her waist with strings, to bed. She had her own cot in an alcove off the kitchen. Until last year, she'd shared the bed with Hannah, but now there was no one to notice a bulge under her nightgown.

Sally had forgotten it herself by the next morning. Only half awake, she rolled over, and felt the hard ring through layers of cloth. "*Mm?*" The whole golden scene in the Lawtons' parlor came back to her, and her heart flooded with secret joy. She put a hand in her pocket, fingering the circle of the ring.

Sally's joyful mood fled as her bed curtains were yanked open. "Early to bed and early to *rise*," said Felicity Gifford.

Sally started guiltily, and her heart thumped. Although her hand was under the bedcovers, she slid it away from the ring. She must give it back to Kitty, today — this morning.

No — not today. This was Sunday, and the Giffords would be at church all day. So would Kitty and her family, only at a different church. Sally would just have to be very, very careful.

All day Sally worried about the ring in her pocket. Sitting in church, she imagined it falling out of her pocket with a clunk and rolling across the wooden floor, right to the foot of the pulpit. She could hardly keep herself from touching her pocket over and over to make sure the ring was safe. At home, she had a wild fancy that the ring could shine even through her pocket and her skirt. Surely the gleaming gold would catch Mother Felicity's eye!

Bedtime came at last, and with her curtains drawn, Sally relaxed for the first time that day. She lay back, holding the ring, and floated on thoughts about how her life had changed.

The change had begun one afternoon in April, when trees had not yet leafed out, but the grass had turned bright green. Sally's stepmother sent her to the well for a pail of water. The well was actually on the Lawtons' land, at the bottom of their orchard, but the Giffords had a deeded right to draw water from it. Sally often met the Lawtons' kitchen maid or groom at the well.

That day, however, a girl in a pink flounced dress sat on the edge of the well, her face in her hands.

"Oh," said Sally, surprised.

The girl looked up, and Sally recognized Kitty Lawton.

She'd never seen the other girl with such red, swollen eyes, though.

Kitty forced a smile. "Oh — good day. You're Sally Gifford, aren't you?" She sniffled. "I came for a drink because . . . because the water straight from the well is so cool and fresh."

"Oh," said Sally again, glancing at the dipper hanging by the well. It looked perfectly dry. Shrugging and smiling, she began to lower the bucket into the well.

"Some girls can be so hateful," Kitty burst out.

Sally, even more surprised, glanced over her shoulder at the Lawton girl. Kitty went on in a low, trembling voice, "I wish with all my heart that dear Governor Hutchinson and kind Peggy Hutchinson had not gone to Milton. *Peggy* is a true friend. *She* would speak to me. She would invite me to sit with her at the concert."

"The concert at Faneuil Hall?" asked Sally. She'd seen a handbill for today's concert.

"Yes, it was to be a lovely afternoon, and then I saw the Cushings at the door and waved to the girls. And they" — her voice broke — "they put their noses in the air, and they went and sat on the other side of the hall! And Deborah Cushing and I are in the same dancing class! How can they be so mean?"

"Maybe you only thought they saw you," said Sally, hauling up the full bucket.

"Oh, they did see me." Kitty gave a hurt laugh. "And I know why they're snubbing me. They're not the only ones.

It's because Governor Hutchinson is a dear friend of Papa's, and because of the taxes."

Sally didn't know what to say. She'd never heard anyone speak good of the governor of Massachusetts Colony. She felt sorry and embarrassed for Kitty.

Kitty went on, "Papa says, how do they suppose the King is to pay his debts for the French and Indian War? Wars cost a great deal of money!" She paused, as if she had remembered something else to be unhappy about, and choked on a sob. "I wish Papa hadn't gone to London!"

Sally could hardly believe that Kitty, Kitty Lawton of the silk stockings, was confiding in her. Although now, with a puffy and tear-streaked face, Kitty looked less like a princess and more like an ordinary girl. She was only a year or two older than Sally.

Swinging the bucket over the edge of the well, Sally handed Kitty the dipper. "Here's your fresh water."

Kitty looked puzzled, as if she'd forgotten why she'd said she came to the well. Then she nodded and drank, her neck bent gracefully over the dipper.

Watching Kitty, Sally felt a surge of anger toward those girls who'd mistreated her. "The Cushing girls must be cruel and ignorant!" she declared. "A pox on them!" Immediately she clapped both hands over her mouth. "I didn't mean that," she whispered. Smallpox was too horrible to wish on anyone. "My mama died of the pox."

Kitty straightened and gave Sally a wondering look. "She did? So did my mama. Eight years ago this fall."

Sally nodded. "That's when mine died, too."

Hanging up the dipper, Kitty gazed at Sally as if she saw something special about her. "Will you come to tea tomorrow? Please come."

Sally couldn't go to tea the next day, because she had to help Felicity Gifford with the weekly baking. But it wasn't long afterward that Sally stepped into that magical parlor for the first time. As spring turned into summer, Sally visited Kitty more and more.

Kitty, who'd taken music lessons for years, taught Sally to play simple chords on the spinet. In the beginning, Sally was nervous about touching such a valuable instrument. What if she broke it? But Kitty laughed at the idea, and seemed delighted to watch Sally learn. "You have naturally refined instincts," she assured her.

If the weather was pleasant, the girls sat in the orchard and read one of the books from the Lawtons' library. At home, the Giffords' only books were the Bible, the hymnbook, the almanac, and a battered children's primer. But the Lawtons needed a separate room just for their shelves and shelves of books: histories, books about science, books of legends, books of poems, novels. Sally had never seen so many books together, except at the printer's shop.

Some of the stories in the books gave Kitty ideas for plays. The girls made themselves costumes with curtains and sheets, and wove wreaths with flowers from the garden. At first, Sally felt uneasy about acting out plays — was it right to pretend to be someone else? What would Pastor Bacon at the Old South Meeting House say? Plays were forbidden in the town of Boston.

"It's only *public* plays that aren't allowed," Kitty explained. "Why, the Hutchinsons have plays, and they're the most upright family you could imagine." Kitty threw herself into roles, catching Sally up in her excitement. Kitty's favorite role was that of Mary, the tragic Queen of Scots, so brave and noble even as she went to her death by beheading on the scaffold.

Sometimes, when it rained, the girls brought out their stitchery projects. Although Kitty never darned socks, she knew many fine embroidery stitches, and her sewing basket was full of all colors of silk embroidery thread. While Kitty worked at a pillow cover for her father, to give him when he returned from London, Sally sewed a beanbag for Josiah.

Sally's goal was mainly to please her stepmother by doing something nice for her half brother, but she was proud of the way the toy turned out. She stitched a face on the beanbag, and a curled wig, and a coat with gold buttons, and a ruffled shirt.

"It's a gentleman beanbag — and he looks just like Papa!" Kitty squealed with delight. "You clever, clever girl, Sally!"

Sally had never had so many compliments as she got from Kitty. She soaked them up the way griddle cakes soak up syrup.

Lying in her bed that Sunday night in August, Sally was amazed all over again to think how her life had changed.

And maybe it was about to change even more! Sally sensed something coming into view over the horizon, like the very tip of the mainmast of a ship laden with treasure, sailing toward her.

Monday morning, Sally woke up certain that she'd come to a crossroads. Depending on what she decided today, her life could be different from now on. Of course there were things that wouldn't change, at least not right away. Through the bed curtains she could hear her father at the kitchen hearth, rekindling the fire as he did every morning. Soon Sally would have to get dressed, milk Buttercup the cow, and lead her to pasture, as she did every morning. But first, she had a choice to make. What would she do with the ring?

Now that Sally had spent a whole day with the ring in her pocket, her terror of being found out seemed foolish. Besides, Sally saw that if she gave the ring up, she'd be taking a step backward in her friendship with Kitty. They had made a solemn pledge to be sisters at heart, and their secret exchange of tokens sealed the pledge.

Did Sally have the courage to keep the ring? If it was the price of being Kitty's friend, maybe she did. Although Sally was still lying in bed, her breath was short as she felt in her pocket for the ring. She took it out, along with the little leather pouch that had protected the heart-shaped brooch. She slipped the ring into the pouch, pulled the drawstrings tight, and pushed the ring back into her pocket. *There.*

As Sally went about her morning chores, she tried not to

show how excited she felt. But the rest of her family did their chores and ate their mush and molasses with hardly a glance at her. After breakfast, Mr. Gifford and Ethan tied on their leather aprons and went into the shop. Sally followed them with a broom, to make the workshop tidy for her father's customers.

The workshop was a nicer, better furnished space than the Giffords' living quarters; the ceiling was higher, and there was brass hardware on the doors and shutters instead of wooden bars. Sally dusted the curved tops of the chairs on either side of the street door and straightened the piles of newspapers. The Giffords couldn't have afforded two daily papers for themselves, but Mr. Gifford bought them for waiting customers. To please Whig customers, there was the *Boston Gazette*; to please Tory customers, the *Boston Evening Post*.

As Sally swept the floor, Mr. Gifford gave Ethan his instructions for the morning: errands to the blacksmith for nails, to the tanner for leather, and to the printer for today's *Gazette*. Ethan seemed unconscious of the tar spots on his shirt sleeve, but Sally couldn't take her eyes off them.

Had Ethan thrown boiling tar at James? If he hadn't, then how had he gotten tar on his shirt? If he had — how *could* he?

Last year, Sally would have been sure Ethan couldn't do such a thing. Her cousin wasn't a cruel boy, like some in the gangs of apprentices who roamed the streets of Boston. But Ethan had changed.

His looks were different, for one thing. His eyebrows

were thicker and darker, and his jaw harder. He'd grown suddenly taller, as if someone had taken him by his hands and feet and stretched him like molasses taffy. Mrs. Gifford and Sally had let down the hems of his shirts twice since last fall. His breeches and coat were hopelessly too small, and Mrs. Gifford put them away in the chest for Josiah to grow into.

Ethan's toes had stuck out of his shoes, too, until Father had Ethan make a new pair for himself. Father had smiled as he examined Ethan's inexpert work. "Tell folks you're Mr. Mackintosh's apprentice," he joked. Shoemaker Ebenezer Mackintosh was known in Boston for leading mobs, not for his skill in leatherworking.

Besides his looks, Ethan's manner had changed. When Mr. Gifford took him on as an apprentice two years ago, Sally was delighted to have him in the family. He was much more fun than her older sister, Hannah, and he was kind. He'd made the leather pouch for Sally to keep her mother's brooch in, for instance. He'd whittled a whistle for Josiah.

But more and more, Ethan's merry, open expression was overlaid with a scornful gaze he seemed to have borrowed from Harry Cole, the butcher's lad. Sally didn't like Harry, and she didn't like seeing his expression on Ethan's face.

Opening the front door of the shop, Sally began sweeping the steps. While she was brushing a spider web from the shoe sign above the door, Ethan came out. He was jingling coins in the pocket of his leather cobbler's apron.

Ethan gave Sally an absent glance. He would have walked right by, but she held her broom across his way.

"What's this?" he asked with a laugh. "Will you make me pay a toll?" He tried to push the broom aside.

"Did you . . . Who poured tar on James?" Her voice squeaked on "tar," as if her throat tried to hold the word back.

Ethan's mouth opened and closed. He sputtered, "Did I — ?"

"I saw his neck — it's all blisters!" she rushed on.

"You think I — " Ethan's dark eyes flashed. "Did that moony calf tell you I tarred him? I tried to shield him. Got tar on my shirt for my pains. Why, I — " He broke off, waving one hand as if he couldn't bother explaining to her.

Sally's anger drained away, leaving her uncertain. "It wasn't you?"

"And now you're blaming me! James doesn't have the sense of a goose — a Latin School boy, wandering down to the roughest part of town? Some of the apprentices were just waiting for a Tory boy to fall into their hands."

Sally began to explain, "I only asked, because — "

"Many thanks for your confidence in my character, cousin!" Ethan interrupted. "Now pray excuse me."

Her face flushed with embarrassment, Sally stepped aside and watched him go. She wished she could take her words back. James *did* go off into his private world. She could imagine him down at the waterfront, his head full of thoughts about the tides, not seeing danger until he was surrounded by jeering apprentices. Ethan might be unrefined, as Kitty put it, but that didn't mean he was cruel.

4

LIBERTY, PRECIOUS LIBERTY

"Parliament schemes to impoverish our own American tradesmen! To drive them out of business!" The full, deep voice of the Reverend Jonathan Lee, a guest preacher from Connecticut, reached the farthest corner of the Old South Meeting House.

It was Sunday again. Up in the gallery of Old South, the apprentices stamped their feet and hooted to show what they thought of the English Parliament. Down in the pews where the Gifford family sat, there were calls of "Shame on Parliament!" William Gifford didn't shout, but he nodded. So did Felicity, holding Baby Lucy on her lap.

As for Sally, she wished she were sitting next to Kitty in King's Chapel, the Anglican church where Tories worshiped. Like Kitty, Sally would wear a gown with a fine lawn overskirt, and a cap with silky ribbons. The stained-glass windows would cast colored light over the cushioned pews. Grand music would swell from the organ, and the boys' choir would sing like angels.

In Old South Meeting House, a decent Congregational church with clear glass windows and bare wooden floors, Reverend Lee's voice rose and fell. He was preaching on the sin of pride, using the English Parliament and the Massachusetts Colony's governor, Thomas Hutchinson, as his examples.

Sally wished she could do what Kitty did during the sermons at King's Chapel: Kitty read a novel, disguised with the red leather cover from her prayer book. Even supposing Sally had her own prayer book, she wouldn't dare try anything like that. But in her secret heart, she felt safe to tell herself stories.

Sally liked to imagine the fine brick house that Grandfather Downs, her mother's father, would have owned (surely he would have?) if he hadn't died as a young man. *Captain* Downs, Sally had called him to Kitty. Well — she was pretty sure he'd been a ship's officer, at least, not just a common seaman.

In Sally's daydream, Grandfather Downs had *not* died on a voyage to the South Seas. He had survived to become a successful merchant. Sally imagined walking into his parlor, which would have been very much like the Lawtons'. Only, the man in the portrait over the chaise, wearing a silk suit and a powdered wig, was Captain Downs. He loved to shower Sally with presents, and he made sure she had pretty dresses and music lessons.

In reality, Grandfather Downs had died long before Sally was born. There was nothing left of him except the mother-of-pearl brooch, now in Kitty Lawton's pocket.

A new, more satisfying daydream formed like a play in Sally's mind: *In the dining room of a fine brick house on Marlborough Street, the Lawton family sit on the upholstered chairs around their dinner table. They have a guest at dinner today: a refined young girl with blue eyes and dark hair.*

Sally had never actually been invited to dinner at the Lawtons'. If she were invited, she wouldn't have anything nice enough to wear to their polished walnut dinner table. But never mind; Kitty could lend her a dress.

As the second course is served, Mr. Lawton asks Sally to pass the saltcellar. She does so, her sleeve falling back. He notices, for the first time — a birthmark on her right arm! Seizing her wrist, he begins to question her, his voice shaking with emotion. Could it be . . . ?

Sally imagined her eyes meeting Kitty's as Mr. Lawton explained that James had had a twin, a girl baby, who mysteriously disappeared when she was only a few weeks old. This baby had borne just such a birthmark on her right arm. *Now, at the very same moment, tears of joy spring from Kitty's and Sally's eyes . . .* Sally let out a long sigh.

A nudge in the ribs snapped Sally back to the church pew. Her stepmother was shaking her head at her. Sally shrank back, feeling for an instant that Felicity Gifford knew Sally was watching a play. *In church.*

No — it was only that Sally's sigh had announced that

she was not paying attention to the sermon. Trying to look pious, Sally fixed her gaze on Reverend Lee again.

The preacher's broad forehead shone with sweat. He thundered his final line: "It is this that Parliament intends to take from us: liberty, precious liberty!"

The congregation rose and shouted out the closing hymn. Sally sang, too, but her mind was snagged on an obvious problem with her daydream. Sally didn't *have* a birthmark on her wrist — or anywhere else, for that matter. In the novels Sally and Kitty read together, long-lost children were usually identified by a birthmark.

Couldn't a long-lost child be identified by a token left with the baby? An initialed handkerchief, for example. Or a piece of jewelry. Sally's hand slipped into her pocket to feel the gold ring.

That evening, after the Sunday baked beans and brown bread had been eaten and cleared away, Felicity Gifford poured the tea. "I hope they won't call another boycott," she remarked, stirring milk and honey into each mug. "This is the last of our tea."

Sally sipped her mug of the rich, sweet brew. She'd be sorry to give it up, too. Of course she'd still have tea now and then at Kitty's house, because Mr. Lawton would never join the boycott. And tea at Kitty's, served in delicate porcelain cups with lumps of pure sugar, tasted especially delicious.

Everyone loved tea, which was why Mr. Lawton had gone to London this summer, Kitty said. He hoped to make

a great deal of money, if he could get a commission from the East India Company to sell their tea in Boston.

"If we need to boycott English tea," William Gifford answered his wife calmly, "we can drink Dutch tea instead." Some merchant ships, like John Hancock's, smuggled Dutch tea into Boston harbor under the noses of the British warships.

Mr. Gifford sat back in his rocking chair and nodded at Sally; it was time to write the weekly letter to Hannah. Sally fetched her father's pewter inkstand from the shop and set it on the kitchen table, as she did every Sunday afternoon. On market day Hannah's husband, Tom Greene, would cart vegetables from his farm in Concord to the market at Faneuil Hall. He'd sit down to noonday dinner with the Giffords and take Sally's letter in exchange for one from Hannah.

Boston, 22nd August, Sally wrote at the top of the sheet in her neat, clear hand. She wasn't writing on new paper, of course — expensive new paper was only for important documents. This paper was the blank side of a one-page newspaper. The printing showed through a bit, but not enough to make the letter hard to read. *Dear Hannah —*

Pausing, Sally looked over at her stepmother, still sipping her tea. While Mrs. Gifford thought about what she wanted to say, Sally watched Josiah. He was tossing his beanbag in front of Lucy, to make her laugh. "Look, Lucy, the gentleman flies through the air — whoops! He fell on his nose."

"Tell Hannah that Baby Lucy is teething and fretful," said Mrs. Gifford finally. "Ask her if little William" — that was Hannah's baby, named after Father — "has started teething yet. Tell Hannah — Josiah," she interrupted herself, "don't drop the fine beanbag Sally made for you. You'll get it dirty."

Sally thought it was unfair to expect Josiah to keep a toy clean, but she said nothing. When Sally first presented that beanbag to Josiah, Felicity Gifford had looked worried, rather than pleased as Sally had hoped. Felicity seemed to think that the embroidery was *too* fine for a toy.

"Oh, and say, I have a new lace pattern to show Hannah, next time she visits." Felicity Gifford smiled.

Sally felt a twinge of resentment. Thinking of Hannah (unlike thinking of Sally) made their stepmother smile. But Sally wrote down Mrs. Gifford's words. Then she glanced over at her father to see what he wanted to tell Hannah.

"Tell Hannah I'm saving a nice little piece of leather to make my grandson a pair of shoes. She must be sure to trace his feet, when he takes his first steps." Stopping to think, Mr. Gifford ran a hand over his chin, freshly shaven for Sunday meeting. "I wonder if Tom's hand holds him back with the haying. No, don't bother writing that. I'll see Tom himself on market day."

Sally paused with the pen over the inkwell. It made her shudder, thinking of Tom's missing fingertip. He'd had an accident with gunpowder, they learned last week. What had he been doing? He didn't explain. He'd driven his wagon into the Boston market just the same, but he seemed to be trying not to show how much the finger hurt him.

Sally looked down at the paper, wondering if *she* had

anything to tell Hannah. If Hannah were here, what would Sally say?

Sally couldn't tell her sister her most exciting news: that she and Kitty Lawton were sisters at heart. Sally squirmed as she imagined Hannah's baffled face. Sally wasn't sure how she would explain why she'd want a sister from another family, when she already had her own sister by blood.

Then Sally had a happy idea: she could make a toy for Hannah's baby. *I'll sew a beanbag and embroider it for Baby William, like the one I gave Josiah.* Sally finished the letter with love to Hannah, Tom, and Baby William from all of the Giffords.

Sally blotted the wet ink with another old newspaper, and her stepmother held out her hand to read the finished letter. As she ran her eyes over the page, a line appeared between her eyes. "Another beanbag? You mustn't accept any more embroidery silk from Mr. Lawton. We can't possibly pay him back. 'Avoid, above all else, debt,' as *Poor Richard* says."

"But it was Kitty gave me the thread, ma'am," protested Sally. "She said she had much more than she could use."

Felicity Gifford's frown deepened, and Sally's father took his pipe from his mouth as if to reprimand Sally. Children were not supposed to argue with their parents, even if the parents were wrong. Sally forced herself to ask meekly, "Shall I cross out that sentence, ma'am?"

Mrs. Gifford hesitated, then shook her head. "Of course you may sew a beanbag, as you wrote — 'tis a kind thought. Only use our plain linen thread."

Monday morning Sally woke before daylight, sweating in the close air of her curtained alcove. She heard the neighborhood night watchman announce a change in the weather: "Five of the clock, hot and moist." A little later, when Sally led Buttercup to pasture, it was sweltering even on the Common, as if all of Boston were a steamy laundry shed. To make things worse, thought Sally, Monday was wash day.

After breakfast, Sally took Josiah to Dame Hewes' house, where the old woman taught a few children their ABC's. Back home, Sally found Felicity Gifford stirring the laundry in the copper boiler. With the other arm she held Lucy, who was whimpering and rubbing her sore gums.

Sally wished she could walk out the door again and spend the day picking blueberries on the Common and wading in the Frog Pond. But she hefted a basket of wet linen, lugged it into the backyard, and began hanging it up to dry. Shaking out Ethan's shirt, she noticed that the tar spots were still there, although lighter.

Soon the small yard was flapping with wet sheets and shifts and towels, like a cove full of boats hoisting sail. Squinting against the sun, Sally was startled to see a slim shadow on the sheet in front of her. She pushed the damp cloth aside — and there was Kitty in a fresh white dress printed with robin's egg-blue flowers, and a straw hat with a matching ribbon.

Sally burst out laughing with delight. Kitty laughed, too. "Guess what? Papa's home from London, and we're going to Castle Island!"

Before Sally could reply, Felicity appeared dragging another basket, and still carrying the baby on her hip. She didn't seem pleased to see Kitty. "Good morning, Miss Lawton. Sally has work to do."

"Good morning, ma'am." Kitty looked down at the basket of Baby Lucy's linen, with the stains that never quite came out even when it was clean. "Yes, ma'am." She flicked Sally a look that said, *This is outrageous, for you to have to do such drudgery!*

With a curtsy to Mrs. Gifford, Kitty went on. "But Papa wishes me to ask, may Sally come to Castle Island today? He has business at the fort, and James and I are going along with a picnic. We would like so much to bring Sally with us."

"Oh! May I, please, ma'am?" exclaimed Sally.

Even as the words left Sally's mouth, she thought it would have been better to say nothing. Felicity Gifford and the baby both looked at her with faces red from the heat. The hair escaping from their caps clung damply to their cheeks. If Lucy were old enough to talk, Sally was sure *she* would have said "No," just out of spite.

Her stepmother gave Kitty a thin smile. "I'm sure Mr. Lawton must have a *great deal* of business to conduct with Colonel Leslie. But Sally has a great deal of business here, and I can't spare her. Pray thank your father most kindly for me," she added.

"Oh. I see," said Kitty. "Yes, ma'am." With a shrug and a sorrowful roll of her eyes to Sally, she curtsied again and left.

Sally burst out, "Oh, ma'am, may I not go just this

once? I'll finish the laundry in the next half hour!" To prove it, Sally grabbed handfuls of damp linen and began hanging it at double speed.

Felicity Gifford returned to the kitchen without answering, but she reappeared a short while later and surveyed Sally's work. The baby was now nodding sleepily against her mother's shoulder, and Mrs. Gifford looked a little less cross. "Watch what you're doing, Sally," she said. "Haste makes waste. You'll drop the linen in the dirt."

"Yes, ma'am." Sally picked an apron from the basket and shook it out with great care.

Her stepmother went on, "I can't understand why you're so eager to hobnob with the Lawtons. Aside from the fact that they're carriage folk and we're not, Edmund Lawton is the worst kind of Tory, hand in glove with the customs commissioners and the governor. Don't you know that? The less we have to do with them, the better."

"But Father's glad enough to make shoes for them, isn't he?" Sally tried to keep her tone sweet and respectful. "Mr. Lawton might not order any more shoes from Father, if we're unfriendly."

Her stepmother sighed. Sally kept her eyes fixed on the laundry and held her breath.

"I suppose you may go with Kitty today," said Felicity Gifford in a milder tone. "One of us may as well get out of the heat." As Sally started to burst out with thanks, Mrs. Gifford added, "But only if you'll be home in time to fetch the cow."

5

CASTLE ISLAND

Boston Harbor lay still and glassy, and the men rowing Mr. Lawton's barge toward Castle Island let the outgoing tide do half the work. Even out on the water the air was heavy and warm, laden with odors of stale fish and of refuse from the breweries and tanneries at the shore. The barge slid past the British warship *Captain*, Admiral Montagu's flagship, and then through a fleet of fishing boats returning from their early work. Spotting her Uncle Frank out on his boat, the *Sarah D*, Sally waved to him.

Uncle Frank lifted a hand in reply, but he squinted in a puzzled way. He didn't recognize her, Sally realized. Her uncle wasn't expecting to see his niece in Mr. Lawton's barge, especially wearing a summer dress of Kitty's (Kitty had insisted), and with her face shaded by a hat with pink ribbons. Sally had hardly recognized her own face in the looking glass above Kitty's dressing table. At home, there was only one small hand mirror, spotted and dim, that Felicity Gifford used to see if the part in her hair was straight. In Kitty's scroll-framed looking glass, wearing Kitty's pink flounced dress, Sally's image was like a portrait of a young lady.

Sally felt a thrill. Today, she could be a different person — not the girl who'd only hoped to wade in the Frog Pond! Sally gazed over her shoulder at the roofs and church spires of Boston, shrinking with every stroke of the oars. Then she turned her face toward Castle Island, gliding steadily toward her.

A short while ago, when Kitty presented Sally to her father, Sally had felt shy. Mr. Lawton looked just like his portrait in the Lawtons' parlor, except that there were more lines in his face, and his belly strained the front of his vest. Sally had been close to fine gentlemen before, in her father's shop, but that was different — that was in the way of business.

Gazing down at Sally over his ruffled shirt-front, Mr. Lawton had said, "Ah, yes — the shoemaker's daughter."

Sally wondered, as she curtsied, if Mr. Lawton thought she was a suitable companion for *his* daughter. But then he nodded graciously to her and turned an indulgent smile on Kitty. Kitty smiled back, as if she was sure her father would do anything she asked.

Now Mr. Lawton sat by himself in the stern, studying a sheaf of papers. Kitty, in the prow of the boat with her brother and Sally, was in her usual bubbly mood. But James was quiet, and his neck was still covered with a bandage.

Maybe, Sally thought, James was only off somewhere in his thoughts. James's thoughts fascinated Sally. She didn't know anyone else who liked to think about the tides surging from one side of the world to the other, or white light splitting into rainbow colors.

But as she laughed and talked with Kitty, Sally sensed that something was bothering James today. "James, does your burn hurt very much?" she asked.

He shook his head. Kitty explained with a roll of her eyes, "James is *still* mourning for Dr. Franklin's *Experiments*."

James looked annoyed. "It's not a matter of sentiment," he told Sally. "I needed to consult that book today, to conduct my own experiment from Castle Island."

"Did your father lend that book to someone?" asked Sally.

"No," muttered James. "And he never will again."

"Papa flew into a rage and threw it into the fire — oh, months ago," said Kitty. She shook her head ruefully at her brother. "Gone is gone, James! Can you not give it up?"

James didn't answer, but Sally exclaimed, "Your father threw a *book* in the fire?" Books were costly and precious, and Sally couldn't imagine anyone deliberately burning one. Unless it was a sinful book — she had heard of such things. But Dr. Benjamin Franklin was highly respected. He was the Massachusetts House of Representatives' agent in England, a famous inventor, and the author of *Poor Richard's Almanac*.

"Oh, yes," Kitty answered, "along with the rest of Dr. Franklin's books. He behaved shamefully, you know.

Dr. Franklin, I mean, not Papa."

"He did?" Sally had never heard anything but praise for Dr. Franklin.

"Why, yes — don't you know that he sent a packet of Governor Hutchinson's private letters to Mr. Cushing, and Mr. Cushing gave them to Mr. Samuel Adams, and Mr. Adams read them out loud in the Massachusetts Assembly?" Kitty stared at her indignantly. "What if you wrote me a letter, and someone stole it and gave it to the town crier, and he announced your secret thoughts all over Boston? It was like that."

Sally had to agree that was a dreadful idea, for the whole town to know her private thoughts. Still, it was hard to believe that Dr. Franklin had done something really shameful.

"Not only that," Kitty went on, "but Mr. Adams twisted the governor's words and published them, and turned the whole town against him. Now the Hutchinsons stay on their estate in Milton, and we hardly see them anymore."

Sally did remember rumors about the letters this spring, and how angrily people had talked about the governor in shops and on street corners. One of her father's customers brought a booklet of the governor's letters to the shop, and it was passed around a great deal.

James, frowning across the water, spoke up again. "At least I pulled one of Dr. Franklin's books from the fire."

Kitty laughed suddenly. "So you did, but it was the wrong book!" She turned to Sally. "It was *Poor Richard*." She held up her forefinger with pretend seriousness. "'Haste makes waste.' 'Early to bed and early to rise.' 'A stitch in time saves nine.'"

Sally loved the way Kitty made fun of those tiresome sayings, and she giggled, but James's frown deepened. Glancing back at his father, he said in a low voice, "Dr. Franklin may be a Whig, but he's a scientist of the first order."

Kitty made a face of mock admiration and nudged Sally, but Sally stopped laughing. James clearly did feel the loss of the book of experiments; it was important to him.

Turning his back on the girls, James took a spyglass from his coat pocket and pointed it toward Castle Island. Birds, only specks from this distance, swooped in front of the steep bluffs that rose from the island's narrow shore. "A flock of Least Terns," said James. "Black-backed Gulls . . ."

After a moment Kitty got James to give Sally a turn with the spyglass. Trying to act as if she handled expensive spyglasses every day, Sally shut her right eye and held the instrument up to her left, as James had done. She saw the gulls and terns clearly now, but it was the fort that caused her to let out her breath: "Oh . . ."

Fort William's stone bulk loomed above the bluffs. Gleaming brass cannon jutted from the fort walls. Above the watch tower the British flag rippled, displaying its red cross over a red, white, and blue background.

Now that Sally could see the quay and boats at the edge of Castle Island, she realized how big the fort was. It was much bigger than any structure in the town of Boston — in fact, the fort seemed like a town in itself. Sally thought of the walled cities, like the city of Jericho, that she'd heard about in Bible stories.

"What is it?" asked Kitty as Sally handed her the spyglass. "What did you see?" She raised the glass and peered toward the fort. "Oh, look how the flag waves — there must be a lovely breeze up there!"

The barge drew closer and closer, finally sliding into the shadow of the cliffs. They docked, and Sally and the Lawtons climbed the stone steps to the fort entrance. The massive iron-bound gate was shut, but a small wicket door set into the gate opened for them.

As Sally passed through the door, she glanced from under her straw hat at the soldier on guard. He'd looked spruce and military from down below, but close up, she saw stubble on his long jaw. And there was a splotch of — what? Gravy? — on the front of his scarlet coat. His nose seemed to have been broken more than once, and the set of his mouth was sullen.

Stepping into the fort, Sally forgot about the untidy sentry and looked around curiously. The shape of the fort was easier to see from inside its walls: it was five-sided. A bastion guarded by a soldier jutted from each of the five corners. On the parade ground, dozens of red-coated soldiers were drilling. Sally hadn't seen so many British soldiers since she was seven years old.

"Look, Sally," remarked Kitty, "just like James's toy soldiers." They did look like the toy soldiers Sally had seen in a shop window, but she'd never seen James playing with toys.

Sally caught James giving his sister an irritated glance.

Edmund Lawton, ahead of the young people, turned to beckon. "Come, girls; come, James. Colonel Leslie's quarters are over there."

Two of the colonel's aides, their uniforms shining with rows of brass buttons, appeared from the officers' quarters and bowed to Mr. Lawton. He presented Kitty as "my daughter, Miss Lawton," James as "my son, Master Lawton," and Sally as "my daughter's friend, Miss Gifford."

Miss Gifford! Mr. Lawton's daughter's friend! As Sally curtsied, she wondered if the British officers would believe that. Then she glanced down at the skirt of her borrowed pink dress, and she felt herself relax. She didn't look like a shoemaker's daughter. She looked like Miss Kitty Lawton's friend — and she was!

One of the aides escorted Mr. Lawton into Colonel Leslie's quarters. The other, a young lieutenant named Burton, smiled at Kitty. "The colonel has given me the pleasant assignment of showing your party the fort, Miss Lawton."

"I could give *you* a tour of the fort, Lieutenant," said Kitty pertly. "We used to come here all the time to visit our dear friends the Hultons."

"Did you? I would be glad to be educated by you, Miss Lawton," said Lieutenant Burton. "But perhaps your friend and your brother will enjoy the tour. Shall we start with the tower?"

Kitty put up her parasol and took the young officer's

arm. As Sally and James fell in step behind them, James mimicked his sister, pretending to raise a parasol and fluttering his eyelashes at Sally. Sally smothered a giggle.

"That was five years ago, when the mob drove the customs commissioners out of Boston — though the commissioners were only doing their duty to the Crown!" Kitty told Lieutenant Burton as they crossed the parade ground. "The Hultons had to live in the officers' quarters at the fort all summer."

"The Boston mob is a dastardly one, they say," remarked the British officer.

"Oh, yes, they're savages! Before that, do you know what they did to poor Governor Hutchinson? He was Lieutenant Governor then. The mob tore his beautiful house apart, stick from stick! They meant to tar and feather him. Peggy Hutchinson told me she was terrified that night."

"The mob looted their house," James put in, suddenly serious again. "They stole the microscope."

Kitty turned to roll her eyes at her brother. "That's the only thing James cares about in that story: 'They stole the *microscope!*'"

"Not the *microscope!*" Lieutenant Burton chuckled with Kitty. "Why, that's worse than slaughtering the family in their beds."

Sally looked at James. He said nothing to his sister or the lieutenant, but he glared at their backs.

Kitty went back to describing that summer on Castle Island five years ago. "Such fun we had here — games, kite-flying, races! But Mr. Hulton and Governor Hutchinson and Papa and all our friends kept begging the King to send troops. The fall weather was coming on, and we needed protection in town. We were so relieved when the troopships were sighted! I waved a flag, and Papa set off fireworks from the ramparts."

Kitty's remarks troubled Sally. She remembered the British soldiers coming to Boston that fall, too, but not the way Kitty described it. She thought of the day the King's troops had landed at Long Wharf: the drumbeats, the shrill fifes, the measured tramp of hundreds of boots on the cobblestones of King Street.

The Giffords and their neighbors had come out to watch the British soldiers march up to the Common. But no one cheered, let alone waved flags or set off fireworks. Sally remembered how her father stood unsmiling, with folded arms. Sally's sister Hannah, thirteen then, bravely pushed little Sally behind her at the first sight of the Redcoats. As for Felicity Gifford, she clutched one-year-old Josiah as if the soldiers would eat him for breakfast.

Was this what her stepmother had meant, Sally wondered, by asking why Sally would want to hobnob with Tories? Sally was a Gifford. The Giffords were Whigs. And Whigs did not welcome British troops.

Up in Fort William's watchtower, a brisk breeze snapped the ribbons of the girls' hats. The soldier on watch saluted Lieutenant Burton and moved aside to give them a good view. They took turns with James's spyglass. While Sally was waiting for Kitty to finish looking, she gazed back across the harbor. Boston as seen from the fort was a miniature town, with tiny church spires poking the sky and tiny wharves poking the water.

It seemed strange to be outside the town where Sally had lived all of her twelve years. Now and then she went out in the harbor in Uncle Frank's dinghy, and once she'd crossed the Charles River on the ferry. But the harbor and the river were really part of the town. From this distance, out of earshot of the town's clatter and clamor, Boston looked small and not very important.

"Quite a good spyglass you have, Master Lawton," the lieutenant said to James. "If it were a clear day, we could see all the way to England from up there."

"I think not, sir," said James coolly.

"On my honor!" Winking at the girls, the lieutenant went on about how one very clear day he'd spotted his old mother back in Shropshire, leaning from her cottage window and waving to him.

Kitty and Sally laughed. James, however, answered in a patient tone, as if talking to an ignoramus. "I'm afraid that's impossible, sir. You see, due to the curvature of the earth, no object in England could be visible to an observer in Boston, even with the most powerful telescope."

Kitty smiled at Lieutenant Burton. "There's no joking with my brother on scientific subjects." But Sally pictured the globe in the Lawtons' library, and the long curved distance between the Massachusetts Bay Colony and England.

Of course: no one could see *through* a slice of the earth.

The officer bowed mockingly to James. "You have me there, Master Lawton. But you will admit that our sentinels can see every ship coming and going from this port." Lieutenant Burton went on to point out the various islands and channels in the harbor, and then he led them down from the tower.

As they continued the tour, James seemed to forget his annoyance at being teased. He examined each section of the fort with interest, and he asked the lieutenant one detailed question after another. How were the walls of the fort constructed? Was the artillery manned night and day, and were sentries posted at the landing? Where was the gunpowder stored? How many kegs?

The young officer answered James politely, but finally he stopped and looked at the boy with his head to one side. "Questions, questions! If I didn't know your father was a merchant, Master Lawton, I'd wonder if you were a spy."

James looked surprised, and then his lips twitched in a smile. "I didn't mean to alarm you, sir," he answered in a gently reassuring tone. "I was only curious. I'm not a spy."

The officer seemed taken aback, as if he wasn't sure whether James was making fun of him or not. He forced a laugh. Kitty said, "Pay no attention to my brother — he's being annoying on purpose."

As they walked on, James whispered to Sally, "No joking with him on military subjects, I suppose." He looked pleased with himself.

Lieutenant Burton led them onto a bastion and paused in front of a thick iron-bound door. A ring of keys hung from a beam nearby. "Now, this is the guardhouse."

"The guardhouse," repeated Kitty with interest. "Are there many prisoners? Pirates, perhaps? Or French prisoners of war?"

The young officer looked amused. "No, Miss Lawton; we're at peace with France, for the moment. The only prisoners here are a few deserters."

"What will happen to them?" asked Sally. Immediately she was sorry she'd asked.

"Not much to these particular lads," said Lieutenant Burton carefully. "This is only their first offense, so they'll be flogged and then put back in the regiment. But if they try it again, it'll be more serious."

"You mean, they'd be shot," said James.

"Mm." The officer looked uneasily at the girls, as if he hadn't meant to let the conversation get so grim. "Well! That concludes our tour. Now my orders are to escort you to the picnic site."

6

I Wish You Were Here

By the time Sally returned to Boston with the Lawtons, the sun was low in the sky. She'd barely have time to bring the cow in from the Common. Hastily changing back into her own clothes in Kitty's room, she hurried through the Lawtons' orchard to the alley.

Before Sally reached the tree-lined Mall on the Common, she heard a shout behind her. "Sally!" It was Ethan, and he was scowling.

Impatiently Sally stopped and waited. As her cousin came close, she noticed that his shirt clung damply to his chest, and she smelled the sweat and shoe leather of his hot day's work. She couldn't help thinking of Lieutenant Burton in his fresh, crisp uniform. "What are you doing here?" she asked.

"I was on my way to get the cow," said Ethan pointedly.

"Uncle William sent me when you didn't come home for supper."

"I'm sorry that you troubled yourself, but I never promised to be home for supper," said Sally. "I'm fetching Buttercup, just as I said I would."

"You're sorry I troubled myself." Ethan affected a mincing tone. "Oh, my. Ain't she getting above herself. It must be that pink dress you put on at the Tories' house."

Sally felt her face redden. "What if I did?" she snapped.

Ethan gave a short laugh. "Thought you'd sneak off without anyone seeing you acting the young lady, eh? You aren't any better at sneaking than you are at putting on grand airs."

Turning away without an answer, she stalked across Common Street and into the Mall, the leafy public walkway. Ethan was mean and rude. Sally would not let him spoil her lovely day. But she was more upset by Ethan's words than she wanted to admit. Her stepmother and father were bound to be just as unsympathetic.

Instead of going straight to the pasture, Sally took a detour, past the low public granary building, to the burying ground. She stopped in front of a granite slab as high as her knees. Words were carved into the stone: *Here lies the Body of Sarah Gifford, wife to William Gifford, aged 36.*

"Mama," Sally whispered. She'd never called her mother anything but "Mama." When Sarah Gifford died, Sally had been only three years old. And when her father remarried the following year, Sally did not start calling Felicity "Mama." No one except her mother could be

"Mama." From the beginning, Sally had thought of her step-mother as "Mother Felicity."

With a glance around to make sure no one was watching, Sally knelt on the grass in front of the grave marker. She fumbled in her pocket to find the ring. Keeping her hands in her lap, she slipped the ring onto the middle finger of her right hand.

"Kitty has your brooch, Mama," Sally explained. "She's keeping it for me, just as I'm keeping her mama's mourning ring, because we're sisters at heart." Mama would understand; as Sally imagined her, she always understood. Sally pictured her mother admiring the ring with soft eyes, happy that her daughter had such a wonderful friend.

A shout from the direction of the Watch House startled Sally. Her head jerked around, and she plunged her hands into the folds of her skirt. Then she felt foolish, because the air over the Common was thick, and the sun was now behind the trees. No one in the Watch House could have seen the ring, nor would they care about it even if they had.

On the other hand . . . She turned back to stare through the Mall. What if Ethan had followed to spy on her, instead of going home?

Sally poked the ring back down to the bottom of her pocket and smoothed her skirt. No one was watching, she told herself sharply. She had a right to keep the ring, and a right to her friendship with Kitty. Pushing herself up from the grass, she strode defiantly across the Common to fetch the cow.

For several days after the trip to Castle Island, Sally felt grateful to Felicity for letting her go, and she tried hard to be a good stepdaughter. Besides doing chores without being told, Sally made an extra effort to help with the younger children. She played pat-a-cake with Baby Lucy, and one day when Josiah was in bed with a cough, she sat beside him and told him stories.

Josiah's favorite story was one from the Bible about the battle of Jericho. He loved the moment when Joshua's army blew their trumpets and shouted, and the high, thick walls fell down flat. He let out such a shout of his own that he went into a coughing fit, and Sally had to soothe his throat with sassafras tea and honey.

Felicity seemed to notice Sally's efforts. Once Sally overheard her say to a neighbor, "The girl is becoming a positive help, after all." She was more willing to allow Sally to visit Kitty, and Sally was careful to return home on time.

But at the beginning of September, Kitty left Boston. She went to Milton to spend a month at Governor Hutchinson's country estate, as the guest of his daughter Peggy. Suddenly there was no chance that Kitty might appear at the well, or even that Sally might hear music from the spinet if she walked past the brick house on Marlborough Street. At least Sally had the gold ring. She was glad she hadn't given it back.

Life seemed very dull, and Sally didn't feel so grateful to her stepmother. She dawdled over her share of the mending, wishing she could embroider designs with bright silk thread, instead. "A stitch in time saves nine," Mrs. Gifford reminded Sally.

Luckily James rode between Boston and Milton a couple of times a week, so he could hand-deliver letters to Sally. The first one arrived only a few days after Kitty's departure, and Sally eagerly broke the seal and read:

> *The Governor's Residence, Milton,*
> *8th September*
> *Dear Sally,*
>
> *I wish you were here for all the Fun! Peggy Hutchinson is so lively and agreeable, even though she's twenty and the Daughter of the Governor. She invites young neighbors to Tea almost every day, and we play Croquet on the lawn. Sometimes we drive out to the River for picnics.*
>
> *Peggy has a dear little terrier, Fifi. It can sit up, and beg, and bow. A Lady comes to the house to give drawing and French lessons. (To us girls, I mean, not to Fifi!)*
>
> *You must beg your Father and the Wicked Stepmother to let you visit me in Milton. Truly, Peggy says any Friend of mine would be welcome.*
>
> *Write back soon!*

Sally folded Kitty's letter and tucked it in her pocket. Even though she'd looked forward impatiently to this letter, it left her feeling neglected and resentful and full of contradictory wishes.

Kitty ought to understand that a shoemaker's daughter couldn't just flounce off to the country to play croquet and romp with pet dogs. Why, Sally hadn't even visited Hannah and Tom's farm in Concord yet! On the other hand —

Sally didn't want Kitty to think of her as the shoemaker's daughter.

Kitty ought to understand that Sally's parents would never let her go to Milton, but —

Sally would never ask in the first place. The very thought of pulling up in front of Governor Hutchinson's grand residence in a farm wagon, wearing her homespun dress, made Sally cringe. How the servants would laugh at her!

Even Kitty's eager "Write back soon!" was proof of her thoughtlessness. Sally had to plan and scheme for enough privacy to write. If her father or stepmother caught her with the pen and paper, they'd want to see her letter.

When Sally finally found a few moments alone, she hardly knew what to write.

Boston,
10th September
Dear Kitty,
I am not allowed to go visiting, and that is that.

Sally rested her pen above the paper, the blank back of an old *Boston Gazette*. Her mind buzzed with complaints, but she was afraid that complaining would push Kitty further away. Searching for something else to say, she thought of the rumors flying around Boston these days, about something the British Parliament had done. It had to do with a new tax, which naturally no one wanted to pay.

But that wouldn't interest Kitty. Finally Sally wrote down

some odds and ends of neighborhood gossip. The best bit was about a tug-of-war she'd seen between Harry Cole and a stray dog. The dog had clamped its jaws onto a haunch of venison that Harry was delivering for his master, the butcher. Harry finally got the venison away from the dog, but then the customer refused to accept the chewed meat. It served Harry right, Sally thought, and even Ethan had laughed.

Toward the end of September, the rumors from England settled down into a few solid facts. The powerful British East India Company was shipping huge cargoes of tea to Boston, as well as to New York and Philadelphia. By the Tea Act, a law passed by Parliament, the colonies would have to pay a tax on this tea.

At William Gifford's shop, people lingered or found some excuse to drop in, just to talk about the tea tax. Talking made them thirsty, and Felicity often had Sally take them a pitcher of cider. One afternoon Sally found Silas Ward, the tailor down the street, deep in discussion with Abiel Ruddock, a merchant. Her father was sewing new soles on the merchant's shoes.

"It seems that Parliament is determined to break our will," said Mr. Ruddock as he poured himself a cup of cider. "They will not let us have a say about this tea tax."

"Furthermore," said Mr. Ward, taking the pitcher from the merchant, "our loyal Boston merchants" — he made a little bow toward the other man — "won't profit."

Smiling wryly, Mr. Ruddock returned the bow. "Indeed,

the profit will go to the Tory merchants chosen by the East India Company." He sipped his cider and turned to the shoemaker. "Mr. Gifford, what are we to do?"

Sally, impressed with the merchant's respectful tone, paused on her way back to the kitchen.

William Gifford looked up from his workbench with a serious face. "As I see it, Parliament is in the wrong, and we cannot simply give in." He hesitated, then added, "Still, I think we need to use caution. Some of the hotheads in town would like to push us into reckless action."

Sally watched the other men's faces as they listened to her father. The merchant frowned and nodded. The tailor smiled ruefully, and he remarked, "Aye, we must stand fast — but cautiously!"

One evening a few days later, William Gifford came home from the Bunch of Grapes tavern with a troubled brow. "The talk was all about Samuel Adams' letter in the *Boston Gazette*, calling for a "CONGRESS OF AMERICAN STATES."

"States?" asked Mrs. Gifford. "Does he mean the colonies? They are hardly 'states'!"

"States, colonies — in any case, his idea is that each colony ought to send a representative to a meeting and discuss what to do about the Tea Act."

Felicity Gifford snorted. "Mr. Adams makes a great to-do about a simple matter. If we all stopped buying tea, that would be the end of it." And she did stop buying tea, even if the shopkeeper swore it was tea smuggled from Holland.

The Giffords all missed their mugs of the fragrant brew, but no one complained. "Anyone in Boston who tries to enforce the tea tax is a traitor, plain and simple," said Ethan.

"'Traitor' is a strong word," said Mr. Gifford sternly to his nephew. "Harry Cole may throw such insults around, but you want to be more careful."

The next afternoon, as Felicity Gifford began to stir up a cornmeal pudding, she noticed that the molasses jug was missing from its shelf. "Where have you put it, Sally?"

Sally was sure she hadn't put it anywhere, but she grumpily went looking. First she checked the kitchen, where the molasses should have been, and then she went out in the yard, where it shouldn't have been.

But there was the brown jug, on the ground next to the chopping block, and there was Josiah, playing some kind of game. He was talking to his beanbag gentleman, the toy that looked like Mr. Lawton. Sally, curious, stopped on the doorstep to watch.

Her little brother set the beanbag on the chopping block, settling it to make it stand upright. Then he lifted the jug high. "Traitor!" he shouted, pouring molasses over the little man. He scooped up a few chicken feathers from the ground and let them fall on the dark goo. "That'll teach you to sell tea!"

Shocked, Sally lunged at Josiah and cuffed him on the side of the head. "That'll teach you to play such a cruel game. Don't you know that tar burns? That it *hurts*?" She grabbed his arm and hauled him into the kitchen, howling.

"Tell your mother what you did."

But to Sally's further shock, Felicity Gifford scolded *her*. "There was no need to strike your brother, Sally. He was only playing." To her son she said, "You know better than to waste food, Josiah. Bring the molasses back inside at once."

"But ma'am — " Sally took a deep breath.

Mrs. Gifford's attention was on her son, returning with the molasses jug in one hand and his sticky beanbag in the other. "See there — you've spoiled the toy your sister Sally took so much trouble to make for you!" She looked pointedly at Sally. "Just as I feared, it was a waste of silk embroidery thread."

Sally was seething inside, but she bit her tongue. Felicity had already moved on to comforting Josiah. He was crying again, this time about ruining his favorite toy. "There, don't fuss. I suppose it'll come clean in the wash."

Sally thought if she stayed in the kitchen one more minute, she'd pour molasses over both her stepmother and her precious little son. Seizing the broom, she hurried through the door to the workshop. William Gifford stood in the front doorway, talking to a customer, but Ethan was busy at the workbench.

Ethan gave her an amused glance. "You look like you could bite through a boot heel."

"Josiah is a horrid little pig, but *she* thinks he's an angel," muttered Sally. She told Ethan about the "tarring" of the beanbag gentleman.

"Yes, it was wrong of him," said Ethan with an edge in

his voice. "He ought to have played that game in the street, where the real tea merchants could see him. Maybe that would make them think twice."

"You are worse than Josiah!" exclaimed Sally.

"And you don't understand as much as a five-year-old about how the world works. Maybe we can't reach across the ocean and frighten Parliament or the East India Company. But the tea merchants are right here in town. We can make *them* think twice about receiving the tea!"

As their voices rose, Mr. Gifford turned from the doorway, frowning. "Ethan, did I say you could stop working to gossip? Sally, why are you here? You don't sweep the shop in the middle of the day. Go help your mother."

"Yes, sir," said Sally. But as she turned to go she said under her breath, "She is not my mother."

Sally expected Kitty to come home at the end of September, but her next letter announced that she was staying in Milton another week or so. Crumpling the paper into a ball, Sally shoved it into her pocket.

Kitty's letter happened to arrive on a market day, when Tom Greene was in town to sell his produce. At noon, he drove his wagon to the Giffords' house and sat down to dinner with them. Sally tried not to stare at his right hand. The bandage was gone — and so was the tip of his little finger.

Josiah spoke up. "Uncle Thomas, your finger!"

Tom looked at his hand and shrugged. "Aye, that bit's gone for good. Teach me not to play with gunpowder, eh?"

Sally wondered again exactly what had happened, but Felicity Gifford changed the subject, asking Tom if he had a letter for them from Hannah.

Tom's forehead creased with worry. "Nay. Too tired to write. Baby keeps her up at night."

Mrs. Gifford looked worried, too. "And all the harvest work yet to do."

"Aye," said Tom. "Thought I might hire the neighbor's girl to help her."

As William and Felicity Gifford nodded approval, Sally was struck with a happy idea. *A girl to help*. A girl to live with Hannah and Tom — instead of with her family! "*I* could help Hannah," she told Tom. She looked from her father to her stepmother. "Oh, may I go to Concord — to help Hannah?"

Tom looked surprised, but pleased. "That'd be best for Hannah, her own sister," he said. He turned to Mrs. Gifford. "But could you spare her at home?"

Felicity Gifford answered, "I think we *must* spare Sally, if Hannah needs her." Her voice was even, but Sally thought she knew her stepmother's real feelings: she'd be glad to get rid of Sally for a while.

7

A Duty to Rebel

It was a long, jolting ride in Tom Greene's wagon from the town of Boston to the village of Concord. But Sally didn't mind; she was free! The bundle at her feet contained everything she needed: a clean shift and stockings for Sundays, and the novel Kitty had sent her, *The Castle of Otranto*. It was a bright, fresh day, and there were hints of fall color in the trees along the road.

Now and then Sally glanced at her brother-in-law. Tom, ten years older than Hannah, didn't talk much. He wore a farmer's straw hat over his plain hair, which was pulled back and tied with a leather string. Tom gazed steadily over the horse's ears, his big hands holding the reins loosely on his knees.

Recalling Lieutenant Burton at Fort William, his curled and powdered wig and his lively conversation, Sally sighed.

Tom was sturdy, a good provider (as Felicity Gifford was fond of saying), and devoted to his wife and baby. But Sally couldn't imagine wanting to marry a man like him.

Still, Sally had to admit there were things she didn't understand about Tom. What had he been doing with the gunpowder? Unlike James Lawton, Tom wouldn't have been "playing" with it.

In Lexington, Tom paused at the water trough on the village green. While the horse drank, Tom swung down from the wagon. "Hand me the packet of letters, Sally. Under the seat." Sorting through the bundle of papers, he picked out three and walked toward the tavern at the edge of the green.

While Tom was talking to the tavern keeper outside his door, Sally glanced at the packet on the wagon seat. The top letter was addressed to the Concord Committee of Correspondence. Sally had heard mention of the Committees of Correspondence by her parents, and by men who visited the shop.

In Boston, the Committee included important Whigs like Samuel Adams and John Hancock. Apparently there were such committees in other American colonies as well as in Massachusetts. Sally gathered that the committees wrote to each other constantly, mainly about outrageous things that Governor Hutchinson or the British Parliament had done.

Tom swung back into the wagon, tucking the packet under the seat, and they drove on through Lexington. Late in the afternoon, as the wagon topped a rise, Tom pointed out his farm: stone-fenced pastures and fields of grain covering the slope to the river. The reddish-brown farmhouse sat close to the road, and Sally glimpsed someone looking out a front window — Hannah.

As the wagon rounded the house toward the barn, Sally felt a qualm. Would Hannah be happy to see her, or would she rather have the neighbor's girl for help? Sally remembered how often Hannah had criticized and reproved her, before she left home.

Hannah stepped out of the back door, wiping her hands on her apron. "Why, Sally Gifford!" She looked amazed. "I didn't expect to see you."

Swinging down from the wagon seat, Tom put an arm around Hannah. "Look, Mrs. Greene. Sally's come to help."

"Truly, Sally?" Hannah's face broke into a smile.

Immediately Sally felt welcome. Jumping down from the wagon, she gave her older sister a kiss. "Truly, Hannah!"

Inside the farmhouse, Sally had to admire Baby William, kicking and waving from his cradle. She gave Hannah the beanbag she'd sewed for him, decorated with a big *W* in linen thread. "It's very plain," she said apologetically. "Mother Felicity didn't want me to use colored silk."

"I should think not," said Hannah cheerfully. "He'd only put it in his mouth and suck the color out."

Glancing around, Sally saw that the farmhouse was as large as the Giffords' house. The kitchen-living room was actually larger than the Giffords', and a looking-glass hung near the door. Tom must be doing well.

Sally was to sleep in the loft, and she was pleased to have

the privacy. As she climbed the ladder to put her bundle in the loft, she sniffed fragrant drying herbs hanging from the rafters: lavender, feverfew, sage.

That first evening, Sally fell happily into her new role as the helpful sister. While Hannah tended Baby William, Sally got supper on the table. After supper, Sally cleared and washed up. Hannah, sitting back in a rocking chair with the baby, smiled at her. Sally noted dark circles under her eyes — she must be tired, as Tom had said.

Still, under the tiredness, there was a content expression on Hannah's face. Sally remembered Hannah at home as bossy, always scornfully superior to Sally. Now she actually seemed grateful that Sally had come.

When the kitchen was tidy, Sally knelt on the rug, playing with the baby, while Hannah rocked and knitted. Little Will was younger than Baby Lucy, but he moved around much more, inching sideways like a crab. When Sally offered him the beanbag, he examined it with a frown, turning it over and over. Sally had to laugh, because he reminded her of her father, looking over Ethan's shoe repair work. Then — just as Hannah had predicted — Will stuffed the toy into his mouth.

Tom sat by the window, catching the last of the light and reading aloud from the latest *Boston Gazette*. One report was about a whaling expedition — successful, except that the first mate had drowned.

That story made Sally think of Grandfather Downs, who had died at sea. Hannah might know whether he'd been a "good provider" while he was alive, and whether he'd actually been a ship's captain. "Hannah, Mama's family — the Downses — they weren't always poor, were they?"

"No, they weren't poor to begin with." Hannah's knitting needles clicked as she talked. "Grandfather Downs, Mother's father, was second mate on a merchant ship, the *Dolphin.*"

Second mate, thought Sally, disappointed. Not "Captain Downs," then.

"I'm sure he would have become first mate in time," Hannah went on, "except for his bad luck. And it came at the worst time, when he and Grandmother Downs were raising three little ones."

"The little ones — that would be Mama, and Uncle Frank, and . . . ?"

"And the little boy who died," said Hannah. "But here's what happened: On that last voyage, the captain of the *Dolphin* went mad. Mother said it was from sunstroke, but Uncle Frank thought it must have been the unwholesome air on the other side of the world. Who knows?"

The other side of the world. Sally pictured the globe in the Lawtons' library, with its drawing of a little ship under sail in the middle of the ocean.

"At any rate," Hannah continued, "the captain imagined that the crew was plotting mutiny. He punished them by putting them on half rations. Grandfather Downs couldn't bear to see the crew suffer unfairly, and finally he led a real mutiny."

"Mutiny!" Sally was shocked. Mutiny, she'd always heard, was one of the worst crimes possible.

Hannah glanced up from her knitting. "If the captain goes mad, it is the bounden *duty* of his men to rebel. Uncle Frank always said so."

"Tom Greene says so, too." Tom spoke up matter-of-factly, as if the duty to rebel were common wisdom, like the time to plant corn.

Sally looked from Hannah to Tom. She felt an undercurrent to their talk, as if they were agreeing about something else besides the law of the sea. "Then . . . what happened to Grandfather and his mutiny?"

"Grandfather Downs was shot by the first mate," said Hannah, "and the mutiny was squelched."

"*Captain* ought to have been shot," growled Tom.

Sally turned toward him in surprise. She'd hardly ever seen Tom show strong feeling, except for his moony look on the day he'd married Hannah. "Was there a trial, when the ship got back to port?"

Hannah shook her head. "I believe there was a hearing, but everyone who might have testified against the captain was dead." She spread her knitting on her lap to check the stitches. "Poor Grandmother Downs! She had to go to the docks and beg the fishermen for fish heads, to feed Mother and Uncle Frank."

Sally felt disturbed and disappointed, and she wished she hadn't asked about the Downs family. Now, if the subject of her grandfather came up again with Kitty, Sally would have to admit that he was only a second mate.

The following afternoon, as Sally was alone in the farm-house, minding the baby, she sat down to write Kitty. Just as at home, there was a stack of old *Boston Gazette* broadsides to use for writing paper.

> *The Greene Farm, Concord,*
> *3rd October*
> *Dear Kitty,*
> *Thank you for sending the Book. James almost forgot — of*
> *course! — to bring it by. He appeared just when I was leaving in*
> *Tom's wagon. And James handed it to me right in front of Mother*
> *Felicity! I was so glad that The Castle of Otranto was disguised in*
> *the prayer book cover. I managed to tuck the Book into my bundle*
> *before my Stepmother could examine it. Now I only need the time*
> *to read!*

Sally had just as much work to do at her sister's as she did at home, and it was the same kind of work: minding the baby, cleaning, cooking. There was even more cooking to do here on the farm, because of the extra men working in the fields with Tom. Still, Sally felt more willing to work at the Greenes'. Hannah hadn't once complained, "Sally, you've let the mush stick to the bottom of the pot," or, "Sally, I see cobwebs in the rafters still," the way Felicity Gifford did. And she hadn't quoted proverbs from *Poor Richard's Almanac* at Sally.

Posting a letter to Kitty in Milton from the farm was

a problem, though. In Concord, there was no James to act as courier. If Sally had a penny, she could leave the letter at Bennett's store in the village, and they would give it to the coachman on the Milton route. But Sally had no money.

Baby Will gave a whimper, and Sally rocked the cradle with her foot. What else to say to Kitty? Kitty ought to appreciate that Sally had to go to some trouble to get a letter to her. Sally dipped her pen in the inkwell again.

> *I must find a way to post this Letter to you. If only my Brother-in-Law traveled from Concord to Milton, rather than Boston! Tom carries a great many letters, but only between Concord and Boston. He takes private letters for the neighbors, as well as letters for the Committees of Correspondence.*

Sally paused, wondering whether to cross out the last sentence. Sally was anxious to make her letter lively, so that Kitty would want to write back right away. What did Kitty care about the Committees of Correspondence?

Sally herself didn't care, except she wondered if there was a Committee of Correspondence in Milton, or if there were even Whigs in Milton. It seemed possible that someone in the village of Concord, perhaps even Tom, made regular trips to Milton and would be willing to deliver her letter. Possible — but far-fetched. Also, Sally didn't like to ask.

The baby let out a squall. Sally would have to pick him up and take him to Hannah to be fed.

I must close.
Your Sister at Heart,
Sally

By the next day, it occurred to Sally that her work was saving Hannah and Tom the money they would have paid a hired girl. Surely, she told herself, it was not too much to ask for postage for a letter. She brought up the subject as she and Hannah were doing the weekly baking.

"Of course your work is worth something," said Hannah as she punched and turned the bread dough, "but why spend a penny on the post? Only wait until market day, and Tom will carry your letter to Boston."

"But this isn't a letter home," Sally explained. "It's a letter to . . . Milton."

Hannah looked up from the dough in surprise. "Who do you write to in Milton, then?"

"Our neighbor Kitty Lawton. She's staying at — she's staying in Milton just now." Sally didn't like to mention the governor.

"Miss Lawton? The Tory merchant's daughter?" Hannah smiled as if at a joke. "Is Miss Kitty Lawton now a friend of yours?"

"Yes, she is." Sally felt uncomfortable, trying to explain this friendship to her sister. "She's been very kind. She teaches me to play the spinet, and lends me books."

"Does she!" Hannah laughed. "Sally, what earthly good will spinet lessons do a shoemaker's daughter?" She

72

shook her head, still laughing. "What do Father and Mother Felicity say of this strange friendship?"

"Mother Felicity thinks it's foolish," said Sally.

"You're an odd duck, Sally Gifford," said Hannah. "Look in the oven to see if the coals are ready for the bread." After the loaves of bread were set to bake, she remarked, "I suppose you could use our credit at Bennett's store for the postage."

So that afternoon Sally carried a basket of eggs and a jar of honey from the farm into the village. In Bennett's store she set the eggs and honey on the counter.

Mrs. Bennett, a tall woman with a long, sharp nose, quickly counted the eggs and made a note in her account book. "Will the Greenes be wanting any goods today?"

"No, ma'am," said Sally, "just a letter to post." She took her letter, wrapped in a second sheet of the *Boston Gazette* and sealed with a dab of pitch, from her pocket.

The storekeeper's eyebrows flicked upward as she glanced at the address. "The governor's residence. I wouldn't think Hannah Greene had any friends *there*."

Sally wished she could have posted the letter without anyone knowing. She shrugged and gave an empty-headed giggle, as if Hannah had written the letter and she had no idea about it. Mrs. Bennett looked annoyed to be deprived of gossip, but she dropped the letter in the postbox and subtracted the penny from the Greenes' account.

෨෬ଓ ෨෬ଓ

As the days passed, Sally grew restless. Nothing happened, here in the countryside! In Boston there was always something happening: customers coming to the shop, people bustling up and down Winter Street, ships sailing in and out of the harbor. Everyone had news to trade: Ethan from his errands, Felicity from her market trips, William Gifford from his tavern evenings. Even Sally gleaned interesting bits from Dame Hewes, when she took Josiah to school.

In the country, news seemed as scarce as roses in January. Sally saw only Hannah, Tom, and Baby Will, and they saw only each other and her. Oh, and she saw the farm workers at noonday dinner — but they were dull fellows who sat down, ate steadily until the food was gone, and got up and left the table.

Only once did any of the hired hands say anything the least bit interesting to Sally. As she set a pot of beans on the table, she caught the words "Fort William," and paused to listen.

"A deserter from the regiment?" asked one of the men.

"Where else?" answered the first speaker. "They say Mr. Barrett found him half-starved in the barn."

A third man spoke up with his mouth full of bread. "*I* say, a Concord farmer didn't ought to be giving work to a British fellow from across the sea before an honest Concord man."

The others grunted agreement, and then the workers stopped talking and got down to the serious business of eating. But their remarks reminded Sally of the guardhouse at

Fort William and the prisoners inside, waiting to be punished for deserting. Why would British soldiers try to leave Castle Island, risking a flogging or perhaps death, and flee into a strange countryside where they had no family or friends?

8

BETRAYED

After several days on the farm, Sally wasn't working as hard and cheerfully as she had at first. She wished she still felt eager to be helpful. But was it her fault, if this dull life made her yawn?

On Monday morning, Sally didn't bounce out of her cot at the first light. As she was stretching and yawning, Hannah called up the ladder, "It's washday! Early to bed and early to rise, Sally!" Just like Mother Felicity, thought Sally grumpily.

Later that day, when Hannah was out tending the chickens, Sally was supposedly minding the baby and supposedly hemming a sheet. Actually, Sally was deep into *The Castle of Otranto*. She did hear the baby fussing on the other side of the room, but she thought it wouldn't hurt him to wait a little. She *had* to finish that chapter . . . and the next chapter . . .

By the time Sally picked up Will, he was screaming, and he screamed all the way to the henhouse. He quieted immediately as Hannah let him nurse, but she frowned at Sally. "What were you doing, to let him cry so?"

"I'm sorry," mumbled Sally. She *was* ashamed about letting the baby cry. But she was even sorrier that Hannah was turning back into the disapproving older sister. Sally promised silently to be more helpful and thoughtful from now on.

That afternoon thunderclouds appeared over the hills, and Hannah and Sally rushed outside to gather the laundry spread on the bushes to dry. The first fat raindrops splashed on the sisters' heads as they ducked into the kitchen with arms piled high, laughing. "In the nick of time!" said Hannah. "How did I manage before you came, Sally?"

Sally, relieved that Hannah seemed pleased with her again, began folding the sheets with her sister. Sally was the same height as Hannah now, and they worked together in an easy rhythm.

Hannah set a folded sheet on the table with an expert flip and held out her hands for the next one. "Sally Gifford, you've grown quite helpful since I left home."

Sally felt warm; she couldn't remember when her sister had ever given her such a compliment. "Hannah Greene, you've grown quite agreeable since you left home!" Her sister smiled and shrugged, as if to admit she'd been bossy.

"You used to be almost as much of a shrew as Mother Felicity," Sally dared to add.

Hannah's smile faded. "Hush, don't call her names. It's

ungrateful to talk about Mother Felicity that way. She gave us a mother's care, even though we weren't her children."

"She had to feed us and clothe us," Sally shot back, "but she doesn't love us the way Mama did, or she wouldn't scold so much."

"She does scold a bit," said Hannah, "but so did our own mother. Mothers have to scold, to make the children mind."

"*Mama* scold?" exclaimed Sally. "She did not! Why, she was the fondest, dearest mother. I remember!"

Hannah gave her a cool look. "You remember as a child of three. Our mother indulged you then, only because you were little. She was strict with me, and she would have been so with you as you grew older." She snapped the wrinkles out of a shirt and picked up a neckerchief of fine linen. "I must iron this," she remarked to herself, "to wear it to Sunday meeting with my cameo brooch." She looked up at Sally. "Did you bring the mother-of-pearl brooch with you from home?"

Sally started guiltily. "No . . ." She tried to come up with a reason for not bringing the brooch, other than that it was in Kitty Lawton's possession. Without thinking, she laid her hand on her skirt to feel the gold ring in her pocket, then jerked her hand away.

However, Hannah didn't seem suspicious. "Just as well not to risk losing your brooch on the journey," she said.

Hannah had dropped the argument about their mother, but Sally felt wounded, as if Hannah had jabbed her in a tender place. Turning her face away, she hugged in memory the day she'd visited her mother's grave. She felt again the gentle love surrounding her as she shared her secret. *That* was Sally's Mama, no matter what Hannah wanted to think.

The next day Sally resolved to be helpful and pleasant with her sister, but not to try to confide in her. Hannah was not a *friend*, after all, like Kitty. Hannah refused to understand about their mother and stepmother — Kitty understood perfectly.

That afternoon Sally worked with Hannah in the kitchen garden, while Baby Will napped in a basket hanging from a nearby oak tree. As Sally and her sister picked beans, a neighbor's boy on horseback stopped by the Greenes' farm. "A letter for you, ma'am," he said to Hannah. "Mrs. Bennett asked me to bring it from the village and save you the bother." He jogged off down the cart track.

Hannah, addressed as "ma'am" — that still sounded odd to Sally. But her sister must be used to it. Hannah's attention was all on the creamy folded paper sealed with red wax. "Why, this is the governor's seal." Her face was suddenly serious — frightened, Sally thought. "Who could be writing Tom from Governor Hutchinson's estate?"

"I think it's a letter for me," said Sally. But Hannah only gave her a puzzled glance, as if that was a nonsensical thing to say. She pulled open the letter.

Hannah's eyes flicked over the page. "Why, this *is* a letter to you." She turned the letter to examine the outside again. "It's addressed 'To Miss Sarah Gifford, the Greene Farm,

Concord.'" She flipped back to the inside. "'Dear Sally' . . . and it's from 'Kitty, your Sister at Heart'?" She gave Sally a sharp look.

"Give me my letter!" Sally reached for it, but her sister whirled away, bent over the unfolded paper.

As Hannah kept on reading, her back straightened. She's angry, thought Sally. Something was wrong. Could Hannah be *that* angry because Sally was such good friends with Kitty? Sally had expected her to be disapproving, maybe hurt — but not *furious*.

Finally Hannah turned and lifted her head. "How could you, Sally?"

"How could I — What do you mean?"

For answer, Hannah threw the letter at her. Sally picked it up and read:

If you cannot come to Milton, I am glad you are in Concord, at least, in the wholesome country Air. Besides not wanting to leave my dear Friend in Boston, I was worried that you might take ill. After all, Papa sent me out to the Countryside expressly so that I would not catch a Fever.

Surely there was nothing for Hannah to get angry about here. Sally read on:

Your Heart is close to mine. (That is a double meaning!)

Sally smiled. She was sure Kitty meant that she was wearing Sally's mother's brooch, probably pinned to her chemise, out of sight. Glancing uneasily at her sister, Sally felt the smile leave her face. She didn't see how Hannah could guess the double meaning, but she wished Hannah hadn't read that line.

> *Your sister at heart,*
> *Catherine Lawton*
> *P.S.: Here is a poem I wrote:*
> *Though Breezes soft the spirits may beguile*
> *And country Vistas lovely stretch for many a mile*
> *But oh! I long my Sister for to see*
> *And merrily chat as we sit at ease and sip our Tea.*

That was a silly poem, thought Sally, but still nothing to send Hannah into a rage. Then her gaze fell on the very last bit:

> *P.P.S: Pray do not write to me on <u>Boston Gazette</u> papers again. When Papa came to Milton yesterday, he noticed the back of your Letter on my lap-desk. He seized the Letter up, declaring that he would <u>not</u> bear the sight of that d — n'd Whig broadside full of that rascal Samuel Adams' mischief-making, etc., etc. Then he discovered your Letter on the other side and read it, although I asked him to give it to me, and he flew into an even worse Temper. I believe it was what you wrote about your Brother-in-law carrying messages for the Committees of Correspondence.*

Sally's heart sank. She raised her eyes to Hannah's stony stare. "What did you tell her about Tom?" demanded Hannah.

"N-nothing . . ." Confused and nervous, Sally could hardly remember what she'd said. "I *wished* that Tom delivered messages to a Milton Committee of Correspondence — but I didn't write that!"

"Evidently you wrote something very much like that," Hannah snapped. "How could you inform on your own brother-in-law?"

"*Inform?* No, I didn't!" Sally was horrified. "I was only explaining to Kitty why Tom couldn't — "

Hannah cut her off with a scornful sound. "If you don't understand why you shouldn't share Tom's business with a Tory like Mr. Lawton, dear friend of Governor Hutchinson and all the customs commissioners — " She gave a short laugh. "No one could be that stupid!"

Sally tried again to explain, but Hannah acted as though she didn't hear, and Sally's voice trailed off. They finished picking the beans in silence.

Sally had never seen Hannah this angry. She told herself that the quarrel would blow over, but suppertime came without Hannah speaking to her sister again.

While Sally set the table for supper, Hannah went out to meet Tom at the well. Through the window Sally watched Hannah talking as Tom washed his face and hands. Sally couldn't hear what they were saying, but Hannah nodded toward the house several times.

When Tom came into the house, he looked at Sally thoughtfully, without returning her smile. They must have been talking about her. Supper was an uncomfortable meal, with only the baby babbling cheerfully.

Afterward Hannah sat down to knit while Sally washed up. Tom opened the almanac, but he didn't read aloud. As Sally scrubbed the pot, Hannah spoke over her shoulder. "You might as well go back home tomorrow, when Tom takes the squashes to market."

Sally was so shocked that she wasn't sure Hannah was talking to her. "Back home?" she repeated. She couldn't see her sister's expression, and Tom kept his gaze on the page.

"Yes, we think it's best," said Hannah.

Leaving the dishpan, Sally went to stand in front of Hannah. "But I came to help! There are still the grape preserves to put up, and the mattress stuffings to change, and . . ."

"You did help," said Hannah, pushing her knitting along on the needles, "and I thank you for that. But we can't trust you now."

We can't trust you. The words stung Sally like a slap, and she rolled her hands in her apron as if to protect herself. "Please, I'm sorry about the letter. I should have thought. I won't say anything — "

"What you wrote the Lawton girl wasn't so important in itself," Hannah said more quietly. "But it showed how careless you are with our private business."

"I know you didn't mean to inform on me," Tom put in, "and I know it was an accident that Mr. Lawton read your letter. But you're friends with the Tory girl, you see? Accidents are bound to happen."

Hannah let her knitting rest in her lap and looked

straight at Sally. "I don't suppose you want to give up your 'sister at heart,' Kitty Lawton."

Sally flushed at Hannah's sarcastic tone. "No," she said, "I *don't* want to give up my friend. I don't see why I should. I think I'm very lucky to associate with such a family as the Lawtons."

"Such a family as the Lawtons," repeated Hannah. She and Tom exchanged a glance. "The Tory girl means more to you than your own kin?" There was a catch in Hannah's voice. "Oh, Sally! Aren't you *proud* that your father is a Gifford, and your mother was a Downs? The Giffords and the Downses may not be wealthy, but our families have always been respected in Boston. Haven't you ever noticed how people come into Father's shop just to get his opinion about this or that?"

"Of course I have," said Sally indignantly, although she'd only noticed it the other day. "That has nothing to do with giving up my friend! Can't *you* see how mean it would be of me to turn on her, when she's been so kind to me? Kitty shares her spinet, her books, her embroidery silk, all the refined things I could wish for — she takes me on outings — "

Hannah threw up her hands, as if it was useless to argue with Sally. "It's best we ask the Wheelers' girl to come help me." Tom nodded.

Sally bit her lip. She was too proud to plead any more. She went back to the dishpan, finished her work, and climbed up to the loft without saying goodnight.

❧❦ ❧❦

The next morning, during the long silent ride back to Boston, Sally wondered how she'd explain to her family that Hannah had sent her home so soon. But no one even asked.

As Sally walked into the kitchen with her bundle, Felicity was combing Josiah's hair with one hand and holding Baby Lucy away from the fireplace with the other. Before Sally could say "Good morning, ma'am," her stepmother exclaimed, "Sally! The answer to my prayers. Take your brother to Dame Hewes while I settle the baby."

Josiah, too, seemed delighted that Sally was back. "Sally, listen how I know my ABC's!" On the way to Dame Hewes', he recited the entire alphabet to her six times.

When Sally returned to the house, Baby Lucy chortled and held out her arms to her half sister. Sally amused Lucy with a clapping game while Felicity Gifford chopped meat for the stew pot.

Felicity wanted to hear the news from Concord. How was Baby William doing, and did Hannah like Felicity's lace pattern? Mrs. Gifford seemed in a better mood than she'd been a week ago. Sally thought it must be the change in the weather; the past week had been mostly clear and dry, with a morning chill.

Sally kept expecting her stepmother to question her about her early return. But Felicity, it turned out, thought she'd guessed the reason. "I'll warrant your sister didn't like your saucy ways, either," she said with a chuckle. "Now: after you put Lucy down for a nap, there's mending to be done." She pointed out a pile of stockings on top of Sally's work basket.

When Sally looked into the shop, her father exclaimed, "Sally, back so soon?" But he thought he knew the reason, too. "Isn't that like Hannah, to fret about taking you away from us too long!" He patted Sally's shoulder.

Ethan, who'd looked after Buttercup while Sally was away, grinned broadly. "That balky, stupid cow is yours again, and welcome to her!"

With all the family glad to have Sally back, she was glad to be home, too. But she was still afraid that Tom might tell her father and stepmother what she'd done. However, at the midday dinner he was his usual calm, quiet self. Sally stole glances at him across the table. She still didn't really understand what he and Hannah were worried about.

Yes, Sally had as good as told Mr. Lawton that Tom was a Whig. But surely that wasn't a *secret*? Even William Gifford, who tried not to offend his Tory customers, didn't make a secret of having Whig sympathies.

Sally could only guess that the danger to Tom was in the letters he carried for the Committees of Correspondence. Were they . . . treasonous? If they were, and the governor discovered that, Tom could be arrested on one of his trips to town. The penalty for the crime of treason was death.

Sally tried to imagine the Boston magistrates arresting Tom, but she didn't think they would. The ones she knew were all Whigs. Would Colonel Leslie send soldiers from Fort William into Boston to seize Tom? The British navy used to seize men and boys from the docks of Boston and "impress" them into service on their warships. One of Ethan's uncles, his mother's brother, had disappeared that way.

But if the British were going to do something like that these days, wouldn't they already have seized the infuriating Mr. Samuel Adams? Still . . . Sally pictured the iron-bound door of the guardhouse at Fort William, and she shivered.

9

INFORMERS

After what happened in Concord, Sally was extra careful to keep Kitty's letters out of her family's sight. She hid them, along with Kitty's novel in its prayer book cover, in the cowshed. When she had a few minutes to spare, she took them out for private reading.

Now that Sally was close to the Lawtons' house again, she missed Kitty even more. She wished she dared to wear the gold ring on a ribbon under her clothes, as Kitty wore the mother-of-pearl brooch pinned to her shift. Lying in bed at night, Sally found herself taking out the ring and slipping it on. When the smooth, heavy ring was on her finger, Kitty seemed closer.

Once Sally actually fell asleep wearing the ring. The next morning she was up, dressed, and halfway to the cowshed before the weight on her finger nudged her drowsy mind. She froze. In a panic, she almost pulled the ring off. Right in the backyard, in broad daylight, where Mrs. Gifford might have appeared any moment!

Sally took a deep breath and went on into the cowshed. No one but Buttercup saw her slide the ring into her pocket.

Sally was anxious to answer Kitty's last letter, the one she'd received in Concord. But finding writing paper that wouldn't offend Kitty's father was a problem. What could she write on, if not the back of a *Boston Gazette*? The Tory paper, the *Boston Evening-Post*, had disappeared from William Gifford's workshop.

After a day or so, Sally had a little luck: She spotted an old handbill stuck under the wheel of a wagon. It advertised last week's concert at Faneuil Hall.

True, the handbill was brown at the edges and puckered from being out in the weather. And there was a yellow spot, with a distinct doggish scent, on one corner, which Sally tore off. It was a shabby piece of paper to send to the governor's estate, but at least the sight of it wouldn't throw Mr. Lawton into a rage.

The letter itself was short. Sally wanted to complain to Kitty about Hannah sending her away, but she was afraid she might accidentally give away more "information." It still hurt Sally that Hannah had accused her of informing on her brother-in-law.

This time Kitty didn't answer right away, and Sally began to worry that the ugly writing paper had put her off. When James finally came by with a new letter from his sister, it was disappointing. Kitty had only scribbled a few lines about how busy she was with entertainments: riding, boating, musical evenings. It seemed that Colonel Leslie (and his aide Lieutenant Burton) from Fort William were visiting the governor. At the bottom of Kitty's letter, there was no "Wish you were here."

And why *would* Kitty miss Sally, when she had such exciting company? Sally felt that she must write Kitty on proper paper this time, and write something interesting. She knew where to get nice letter paper, but she had to wait for the right moment.

The right moment came two days later. Her stepmother had taken Lucy with her on an errand. Josiah was at Dame Hewes's school. Mr. Gifford — as well as Ethan, Sally thought — had gone to the tanner's. Sally sat down at the small table that served her father for an office in the workshop.

But just as Sally was writing "Dear Kitty" in graceful curves, the shop door opened and in came Ethan. Sally jumped, and a blot of ink fell on the page.

Ethan looked surprised to see her, too. "Hello!" He was dangling a pair of shoes with run-down heels from one hand. "Writing a letter for Uncle William, hm?"

"Yes . . . yes, a letter." Sally tried to sound casual, while trembling to imagine Ethan mentioning this to her father.

"If it's a collection letter, it must be to Mr. Hancock." Ethan glanced over her shoulder. "The ones with the biggest moneybags are the slowest to pay their — "

Too late, Sally shielded "Dear Kitty" with her arm.

Ethan let out a long whistle.

"This is none of your business, Ethan Downs!" exclaimed Sally.

"You sneak." Ethan gave a short laugh. "I don't think Uncle William said you could use his writing paper. Why don't you write to your 'dear Kitty' on the back of a broadside?" He nodded toward the pile of *Boston Gazettes* on the bench. "Oh, that wouldn't be good enough for Miss Tory, would it?"

Sally's face burned, but she wasn't going to explain to Ethan how Mr. Lawton felt about the *Gazette*. "I'm only using one sheet," she answered. "Father wouldn't mind."

That was so absurd that Ethan only gave another scornful laugh as answer. Then, as he sat down at the workbench, he chuckled with real humor. "And you've ruined good paper for nothing. Kitty Lawton's back from Milton — I saw her get out of their carriage this morning." Still laughing to himself, he put a shoe on the last and began trimming a piece of leather to fit the heel.

Hateful Ethan! Sally sat staring at the paper, wondering if she could slice off "Dear Kitty" with a knife and put the sheet back in her father's supply. No, he would notice a short sheet of paper more than a missing piece.

As Sally folded the paper and put it in her pocket, Ethan spoke again. "Sometimes I think you don't understand what the Tories are about. Don't you remember what happened to Christopher Seider?" His tone was sober now, and Sally turned to look at him.

Ethan put the hammer down. "He was the same age as me, you know. He'd be an apprentice today, too, if he hadn't been shot three years ago. By that cursed customs informer Richardson."

"Shot!" Sally exclaimed. "Why did Mr. Richardson shoot him?"

"One thing led to another." Ethan's forehead wrinkled as he sorted out the chain of events in his mind. "In the first place, the shopkeeper next door to Richardson's house was trying to sell British goods. Tea and such, with their infernal taxes. The Sons of Liberty weren't going to stand for that! They put up a sign telling what a scoundrel the shopkeeper was, and they gathered a good crowd in front of the shop to keep customers out.

"It was none of Richardson's business, but he pushed his way through the crowd, ripped down the sign, and began calling the leaders scurrilous names. The Sons of Liberty couldn't let him get away with that, so they followed Richardson to his house."

"Maybe Mr. Richardson thought they would tear his house down," said Sally, remembering Kitty's story about the mob attacking their former house.

Ethan gave her a disdainful glance. "Was that a reason to fire into the crowd willy-nilly? Richardson didn't care if he killed someone, or how old they were . . . We had a good funeral for Christopher, you can be sure of that. Father and I marched in the procession." He frowned at Sally. "Don't you even remember the funeral? It was big doings."

Sally remembered vaguely, but she'd been only nine at the time. Besides . . . "But Ethan, Kitty Lawton had nothing to do with shooting Christopher. She would never hurt anyone."

Ethan sighed and shook his head, as if Sally were unbelievably dense. "The Tories are all of a kind. If they aren't informing on us or shooting us, they're milking us dry. They want to make slaves of us. Governor Hutchinson actually put it in writing. He wrote that he wished to see 'further restraint of liberty' in Massachusetts!" He picked up his hammer and attacked the heel again. *Rap!* "Write *that* to Miss Catherine Lawton."

That night Sally was the first to go to bed. She was still thinking about what Ethan had said, and it disturbed her. He'd spoken of Tory "informers" as if they were just as bad as Tories who shot innocent lads, or Tories who drove families into poverty. And Hannah had accused Sally of "informing" on Tom.

Sally turned over restlessly, remembering against her will that scene in the farmhouse. Hannah had also accused Sally of not wanting to give up "Miss Lawton." Well, of course she didn't want to give up her friendship with Kitty, and she *would* not! Feeling for the ring in her pocket, Sally took it out of the pouch and slipped it onto her finger.

Outside on Winter Street, the night watchman called, "Nine of the clock and all's well. Wind in the west." The men in the neighborhood took turns standing watch; tonight the watchman was Silas Ward, the tailor down the street.

Wearing Kitty's ring made Sally think of Kitty wearing her mother-of-pearl heart. Sally had always loved to gaze at the brooch's shimmering colors. She wondered if those colors had any connection with the rainbow light radiating from James's prism. That array of hues hidden in the white light — it was as if a twist of white embroidery silk could unravel into separate strands of red, orange, yellow, green, blue, violet! Sally would have liked to ask James what he thought about the brooch and its mother-of-pearl colors, only of course she couldn't let him in on her secret with Kitty.

Sally was drifting off to sleep when a sharp sound nudged her awake. She sat up and peered out of her niche. Mr. Gifford, locking the shutters, paused and looked toward the workshop door. Ethan, halfway up the ladder to the loft, also stopped to listen.

Knocking. Knocking outside the workshop, at the street door. Could it be a customer? But surely shoes were never urgent enough to roust a family out of bed.

Taking a candle from the table, Mr. Gifford carried it into the workshop. Ethan backed down the ladder and waited. Mrs. Gifford poked her head, already wearing a ruffled nightcap, out of the bedroom door.

Sally heard her father ask a question. Then there was a scraping sound as he lifted the bar to open the street door. A man's voice, polite but serious. Mr. Gifford answering: "You'd best come in."

Sally sat up in bed. As the two men entered the kitchen, her father's raised candle showed a gentleman behind him, wearing a starched white linen neckcloth outside his fawn-colored coat. Edmund Lawton. Sally slid back down under the covers, afraid — of what?

"I must apologize for disturbing you at this late hour, Mr. Gifford," said Mr. Lawton, "but something strange and distressing has come to my attention."

Looking mystified, William Gifford gestured toward a kitchen chair, inviting the other man to sit.

"Thank you," said Mr. Lawton, "I prefer to remain standing. I have reason to believe that your daughter has taken — has in her possession, that is — something belonging to our family."

Sally froze. Her heart seemed to thump in her throat, and the quilt covering her felt very thin.

"What do you mean, sir?" asked Mr. Gifford. "Sally? You say my Sally has taken — Sally! Get up at once!"

"Something of considerable value," added Mr. Lawton.

"Of considerable — " Mrs. Gifford gasped. "What is it? What does he mean?" Behind her, Josiah called sleepily, "What did Sally do?"

With all her might Sally willed herself to melt through the back of the alcove. Instead, she had to creep out of bed. Her father lifted the candle toward her. There was a shocked silence, and then Ethan exclaimed, "Sally Gifford, you're a greater fool than I thought."

In the candlelight, the gold mourning ring on Sally's finger shone like a beacon.

10

An Unnatural Daughter

Mr. Lawton did not stay much longer. Sally dropped the precious ring into his hand; he produced the mother-of-pearl brooch from his waistcoat pocket. Unthinkingly Sally held out her hand for the brooch, but her father took it instead.

"We need say no more about this, eh?" said Mr. Lawton to Mr. Gifford. He stepped toward the workshop, and Mr. Gifford followed him with the candle to light the way. "I'll leave your daughter to your discipline."

William Gifford shut the street door behind his visitor and let the bar fall. "And your daughter to yours," he muttered.

Then Sally's father and stepmother sat her down at the kitchen table. Ethan was ordered to bed, but Sally knew he could hear everything from the loft. Probably Josiah was listening from the bedroom, too.

Mr. and Mrs. Gifford shot question after question at Sally: How could she accept such a valuable piece of jewelry from Kitty? Didn't she know it wasn't really Kitty's to give away? Hadn't they made it clear to her that they didn't want to be indebted to the Lawtons?

Worse, how could Sally give away her one remembrance of her poor dead mother? Did she love the neighbor girl more than she loved her own Mama? What an unnatural daughter!

Sally stammered and stumbled as she tried to answer. "I didn't really *take* the ring — it was only that Kitty wanted me to keep it for her, and I wanted her to keep the brooch, because . . ." Facing her parents, Sally couldn't bring herself to say, "Because we are sisters at heart." She shivered in her nightgown and bare feet. Mama might have understood, but Mother Felicity and Father clearly would not.

Sally tried not to look at Felicity Gifford. The combination of her nightcap and braids with her outraged expression should have been funny, but instead it made Sally feel ashamed. As for her father, Sally noted in miserable glances how old he looked tonight. The front half of his scalp was almost bald, and there were deep grooves from his nose to the corners of his mouth.

Mr. Gifford ordered Sally to recite the Ten Commandments, which of course she'd learned by heart at school. He made her repeat the eighth: "Thou shalt not steal," as well as the fifth: "Honor thy father and thy mother."

Felicity Gifford told a few choice stories — true stories —

about thieving girls and women in Boston. They'd all come to bad ends, either in the brothels by the docks or on the scaffold. Sally wanted to put her hands over her ears.

Finally Mr. Gifford interrupted his wife in a heavy voice. "Sally, you know I must punish you." Sally nodded. He pushed back his chair and lifted a strap from a peg near the back door.

It was almost a relief for Sally to follow her father out to the yard. She turned her back without being told and braced herself for the blows. *Thwack*. After each lash Father had her repeat, "I will not steal. I will honor my mother."

Then it was over. As Sally crawled into bed, her back smarted, but Father hadn't strapped her that hard. What really hurt was that in Father's eyes, she had committed those sins. Lying awkwardly on her stomach, Sally protested to herself. *I didn't really steal! I didn't really dishonor my mother!*

Now that Sally was alone with her thoughts, another painful matter occurred to her: Why had Kitty betrayed their secret pact? Sally had been willing to sneak costly paper from Father and spend Hannah's egg money for the sake of her sister at heart. Couldn't Kitty even keep a secret for her?

The next morning, after leaving the cow in the pasture, Sally stopped by her mother's grave. "Mama," Sally whispered, "I didn't steal the ring, did I? Kitty *gave* it to me to keep for her. And I didn't dishonor you, did I, when I gave her your brooch to keep for me? I didn't break the Commandments."

It made Sally feel a little better to explain things to her

mother . . . except that she couldn't help remembering what Hannah had told her. Hannah had said Mama was strict. She claimed that Mama had scolded, as their stepmother did. She didn't scold *me*! protested Sally silently. She willed herself to imagine only the Mama who cuddled three-year-old Sally on her lap, singing a lullaby.

Walking back home by way of the Mall, Sally was pulled out of her troubles by the brisk music of fifes and drums. She caught sight of the militia — the Boston men ready to be called up in an emergency — marching on the green. Colonel John Hancock was training them. They weren't as polished in their drill as the British soldiers at Fort William, thought Sally. Still, in their smart blue uniforms (paid for by wealthy Mr. Hancock, it was said), they made a fine show on the Common.

Sally sighed and walked on. She wondered what her father would do with the heart-shaped mother-of-pearl brooch. He wouldn't give it away or sell it, would he? He might give it to Hannah, the good daughter — although Hannah already possessed the cameo that Father had given Mama as a wedding present. Probably Father had locked the brooch in the cabinet in the workshop, with his other valuables.

That first day after the dreadful night when Mr. Lawton came for the gold ring, Sally thought she would never feel comfortable with her family again. Her father and stepmother looked at her warily, as if they were waiting to see what sin she would commit next. When Sally took Josiah to Dame Hewes, the little boy announced brightly, "Sally is a thief."

Dame Hewes' eyes widened, and Sally stomped off before the old woman could ask what he meant. Josiah was a hateful little worm, she told herself, and Dame Hewes was a gossip-hungry granny.

Later in the day, when Sally came to fetch her half brother, Dame Hewes pulled her aside. "What's this I hear, Sally?"

Sally couldn't be rude to the old woman, but she looked away from her worried gaze.

Dame Hewes made a clucking noise with her tongue. "I hadn't thought you were a child to bring disgrace on your family; no, I hadn't! The Giffords are well regarded in this town, you know, and a good name is better than gold."

"I must get right back home," muttered Sally, trying to edge away.

The old woman went on. "To be sure, it's been hard times in Boston lately, especially for a shoemaker like your father, and goodness knows we've all had to pinch pennies, but there's no shame in that. As the saying goes, it takes more than fine feathers to make fine birds."

"Yes, ma'am," said Sally desperately. "Josiah," she called into the doorway, "Mother says we must come straight home!"

"But there — I'll wager you'll mend your ways, as long as you stay away from Miss Lawton." Dame Hewes' wrinkles lifted in a smile. "I always thought well of Sarah Downs, and you look just like her as a girl." She patted Sally's face encouragingly.

No doubt Dame Hewes meant well, and really Josiah hadn't meant any harm; he was only excited by the uproar over what Sally had done. But Sally's feelings were raw. For days she was sure the neighbors were gossiping about her, and she shrank from the gaze of everyone she met.

As for Ethan, Sally expected him to be even more scornful of her than before. Gradually, however, she got the sense that he felt sorry for her. Sometimes she caught him studying her thoughtfully, as if he were trying to figure out what was in her mind.

For many days Sally's hand kept wandering to her pocket, feeling for the small, hard circle of the ring. Then she would remember with a pang that she no longer had that special secret. And then she would wonder how Mr. Lawton had come to know about the missing ring. He might have asked Kitty to wear it, and become suspicious when she didn't. But he couldn't have known about the exchange between the girls unless Kitty told him.

Sally's thoughts wavered between reproaching Kitty for betraying her and abandoning her, and worrying about why she hadn't heard from Kitty. What if Kitty's father had punished her harshly for losing the ring? Sally couldn't imagine Mr. Lawton whipping Kitty, but he might shut her in her room. Would he forbid her to play the spinet?

On top of all that, there was a cold little voice in the back of Sally's head, making nasty suggestions. What if Kitty blamed Sally for getting her into trouble? It wouldn't be fair, but how well did Sally really know the other girl? Or Kitty might simply have changed her mind about being sisters at heart.

Sometimes when Sally went to the well, she crept into the Lawtons' orchard, just far enough to see the windows at the back of the house. Once she glimpsed a figure at Kitty's bedroom window, but it was only the stout silhouette of Mrs. Knowlton.

After a week or so, Sally grew tired of moping around, and she began to attack her chores full force. She discovered that scrubbing pots until they shone, or sweeping every last cobweb out of the corners, gave her a certain satisfaction. *I may be an unnatural daughter,* she thought, *but at least no one can call me lazy.*

Gradually Sally's parents seemed to forget what a dreadful thing she had done. Mr. Gifford went back to smiling at Sally and giving her shoulder a pat as she swept his shop. And Mrs. Gifford actually praised Sally for a neatly darned stocking. "I couldn't have mended it better myself," she said, holding the heel up to the light. "This almost makes up for yesterday's scorched mush."

The days grew shorter, and wind from the harbor swooped up the streets of Boston, shaking yellow leaves from the elm trees. The change in the season seemed to fit a restless mood in the town. Harry Cole's apprentice gang swept through the neighborhood in the evenings — Sally would hear Harry's sharp whistle out in the alley, and then Ethan would find an excuse to disappear until bedtime.

The adults talked more and more about the tea that the East India Company was shipping to the colonies. The merchants chosen to sell this tea in the colonies (at a fine profit) were all Tories. In Boston, they included Richard Clarke and his sons, Faneuil and Winslow, Edmund Lawton, and two of Governor Hutchinson's sons. "How convenient that the governor has found some employment for his idle boys," said Dame Hewes sarcastically to Mrs. Gifford.

"Aye, convenient," said Felicity Gifford. "Especially since the tax on tea will go to pay the governor's salary."

The discussions about the tea went on in Mr. Gifford's shop, too. Often as Sally worked in the kitchen, she heard snatches of the argument on the other side of the door. Some thought there was nothing to get so excited about — even with the tax, the price of the new tea would be lower than that of smuggled tea.

Others were alarmed that the governor's salary would be paid by the British Crown rather than the Massachusetts Assembly. "That means he'll be answerable to the king, not to our elected representatives." Still others wondered what New York and Philadelphia might do about the tea shipments headed their way.

One October night Sally's father came home later than usual from his visit to the Bunch of Grapes tavern. Felicity Gifford was waiting up for him, knitting. Sally was in bed, but still awake.

"The talk was all about the Committee of Correspondence

letter in the *Gazette*," said William Gifford to his wife. "Sam Adams' doing, of course."

"I read the letter," said Felicity. "How shall the colonies force their oppressors to proper terms? he asks. And he answers himself: *Form an independent state, AN AMERICAN COMMONWEALTH.*" She made a disapproving clucking sound with her tongue. "Independence? This is reckless talk. Surely we can resist the tax on tea without going so far."

Mr. Gifford grunted agreement. "Besides, I don't see how the colonies could act together," he said. "Although some at the Bunch of Grapes seemed to think they might, if they had a congress and talked it over. But that would take years! Meanwhile, the tea ships will sail into our harbor in just a few weeks. And only twenty days after that, the cargo must be unloaded and the tax paid, or the customs officers will seize it."

A few days later, early on a foggy morning, Sally had a scare at the well. As she was hauling the bucket up, a cloaked figure dashed at her from the yew hedge. Sally gasped and let the bucket drop.

"It's me!" Kitty pushed the hood back, showing her face. "Oh, Sally, they've been watching me day and night." Her voice was breathless as she hugged Sally. "Can you imagine, Papa has Mrs. Knowlton sleep in front of my bedroom door!"

"I've been waiting and waiting . . ." Sally pushed away to get her own breath back. "I was so worried. How *did* you — "

"They were very mistaken to think I would give up my dear friend!" declared Kitty. "Why, if they clapped me in irons and threw me into a foul dungeon, I would still find a way to escape and meet you!"

"Father gave *me* a strapping, that night your father came for the ring," Sally burst out. "Mother Felicity said I'd end up on the gallows."

Kitty squeezed Sally's hands sympathetically. "Never mind. Remember Mary, Queen of Scots, how brave she was on the black-draped scaffold!" Then she cast a glance over her shoulder at the growing light. "I must hasten back before they miss me." She held Sally at arm's length with an anguished look. "Farewell for now! The hollow in the old apple tree" — she nodded toward the orchard — "will be our post-box."

Watching the other girl fade into the fog, Sally shook her head with a bewildered laugh. Kitty hadn't really explained, she thought as she drew up the bucket again, but it didn't seem to matter now. It didn't even matter that they'd lost the tokens of their pledge, the brooch and the ring. The important thing was that they were still friends.

11

MALIGNANT AND
DANGEROUS PERSONS

After meeting Kitty at the well, Sally went about her morning chores with a bouncy step. Some of the glow from those summer afternoons with Kitty seemed to brighten the gray sky. Even though Sally couldn't visit Kitty, the girls could still escape together into play-acting thrilling roles. Kitty, held captive by the lord of the castle, was like Princess Isabella in *The Castle of Otranto*. Sally was like brave, tragic Mary, Queen of Scots, beheaded by her cruel cousin Elizabeth.

At first the notes Sally found in the hollow tree, and the notes she left there, carried on their private games and dramas. Sally wrote a long poem, drawing little pictures to go with it, about a voyager who was shipwrecked on a tropical island and discovered buried treasure. Kitty wrote as if she were really a prisoner in a castle, sending messages to Sally by a friendly tame raven that perched outside the bars of her window.

Meanwhile, angry talk against the tea agents, on the streets and in the newspapers, grew louder and louder. On the morning of October 18th, as Sally swept the shop, she read an article in the *Boston Gazette*. The writer recommended that when the tea arrived, it ought to be shipped straight back to England — and the tea merchants with it.

That same afternoon, Sally caught sight of James on his way home from school. His nose was red and swollen, and his jacket was torn. She called to him, but he trudged on. "Better not talk to me," he muttered over his shoulder. "I'm a filthy Tory."

Sally found out what had happened from Kitty's next letter: The boys at school had beaten her brother. Sally was shocked. It was one thing for Harry Cole's apprentice gang to ambush a rich boy. But she wouldn't expect James's classmates at the Latin School to attack him.

A few days later, as the Giffords ate breakfast, Sally watched Ethan ladling cornmeal mush and molasses from his wooden bowl into his mouth. Something about his hands caught her attention.

Ethan's hands never looked entirely clean; like Mr. Gifford's, they were deeply stained by the shoe leather he worked with. But today they looked dirty in a different way — his fingernails were black.

Sally remembered seeing Harry Cole across the street yesterday. Harry had been delivering a leg of mutton, while

Ethan carried a bundle of leather from the tanner's. The two boys hadn't spoken, but they'd paused and exchanged a look. Harry had nodded, and Ethan had nodded back.

Sally tried to ignore the bad feeling in the pit of her stomach. But it only grew worse as she washed the breakfast dishes, swept the shop, and went to the Lawtons' orchard to check the hollow apple tree for messages. There was a note from Kitty, a very short one: "Look at our front door."

What did Kitty mean? Sally ran back to the alley, down Winter Street to Marlborough, and around to the front of the Lawtons' house.

The paneled oak front door, painted a rich red and topped by a fan-shaped window, was now streaked with black. The polished brass scallop-shell knocker was almost invisible under a coat of . . . tar. Sally put her hand to her mouth. This was a warning to Mr. Lawton from the Sons of Liberty. From Ethan.

Walking slowly back to the shoemaker's shop, Sally noticed a poster nailed to a tree. In fact, looking up and down the street, she saw the same poster on every tree. It announced a meeting at the Liberty Tree at noon on Wednesday — tomorrow. All the "Freemen" of Boston were invited to come and witness an important event. The tea agents, the poster said, would give up their commissions and agree to ship the tea back to England.

Sally found Ethan at work in the shop. "Harry Cole told you to tar the Lawtons' door, didn't he? I think it was cowardly to threaten the whole family."

"I don't do everything Harry Cole tells me to," said Ethan coolly. "But yes, I did slop tar on Mr. Lawton's fine front door. Maybe that'll make him stop threatening *our* families."

"What are you talking about?" Sally demanded. "Mr. Lawton isn't — "

"Mr. Lawton is carrying out Parliament's plot to enslave us. They've decreed that only the East India Company can sell tea to Americans, and at a price that includes their tax."

"But what does that matter, if the price of tea is so low?" asked Sally. "How could that *enslave* us?"

"That's exactly how they scheme to lure us in!" Ethan's forefinger shot out almost to Sally's nose. "The low price is the thin end of the wedge. That's how they plan to shut out the Dutch traders. Then they can raise the price *and* raise the tax. And not only on tea. Why, they can start forcing us to buy all kinds of English goods. Such as *shoes*, for instance."

"Shoes?" Sally looked around the shop. "All the way from England?" She thought of the wide expanse of ocean between England and the Massachusetts Bay Colony. "Why would Boston folk buy English shoes, when Father makes shoes right here?"

Ethan smiled scornfully. "Because the English shoes would be cheaper than Uncle William's, that's why. And what would happen, if no one bought his shoes? Uncle William would be reduced to repair work. He couldn't afford an apprentice — namely, me." He jerked a thumb at his chest. "Why, he wouldn't even be able to keep a cow."

Sally wasn't sure Ethan was right, and she left the shop still angry. And she was still frightened for Kitty. She'd seen a letter in the *Massachusetts Spy*, a Whig newspaper like the *Boston Gazette*, that made her wonder if the Sons of Liberty would stop at threatening. The letter-writer said that if the tea agents refused to resign, they would be "exterminated" as "malignant and dangerous persons."

However, what Ethan had said did make Sally think for the rest of the morning. As she stirred the chowder, she wondered if the tea tax could really lead to such a change in the Giffords' lives. Would they have to make chowder from fish heads, without butter? Mama's family had been that poor, after Grandfather Downs died.

The next morning, Wednesday, at eleven o'clock, all the church bells in Boston began to clang. All, that is, except the deep-toned bell of King's Chapel — the Tory church.

"Mind the baby, Sally," said Felicity Gifford, on her way out the door. "Mind the stew." Sally's father had already locked the shop and left with Ethan for the Liberty Tree.

The tolling bells made Sally's head hum, and she couldn't sit still. Would the tea agents really show up and resign? They expected to make a great deal of money on this tea. And besides, she couldn't picture proud Mr. Lawton meekly giving in to the Sons of Liberty. But if he did resign, it would be a great relief.

The church bells clanged on and on. *Townspeople, turn out!* they shouted. *This is urgent!* Meanwhile, Sally stirred the stew and tucked Lucy in her cradle for a nap.

Finally the bells stopped sounding the alarm, and the clock on Christ Church struck twelve. What had happened? Sally couldn't stand to wait at home to find out. After all, the stew was ready for dinner, and her stepmother hadn't said she had to mind the baby *in the house*. Flinging a shawl around her shoulders, Sally hauled Baby Lucy, blankets and all, out of her cradle.

The baby, heavy with sleep, whimpered a little at the cold air outside the kitchen door. Pulling the wraps tighter, Sally hurried through the backyard to the alley and down Winter Street to Marlborough Street.

Passing the Lawtons' house, Sally glanced up, hoping to see Kitty at a window. But the handsome brick house was tightly shuttered, as if against a blizzard.

Before Sally reached the huge elm tree at the corner of Essex and Marlborough, she began to meet people coming the other way. She caught scraps of indignant muttering: "How dare they?" " — insult to the people of Boston" " — knew they wouldn't show their noses."

A familiar wrinkled face appeared in the disbanding crowd: Dame Hewes, holding onto Josiah with one hand and a neighbor's boy with the other.

Dame Hewes nodded to Sally in greeting. "All the folk in Boston turned out, from Baby Lucy to gray-heads like me, hey? Only not the tea agents. I wouldn't be surprised if this turns ugly."

More and more people were leaving the square, and Sally knew she'd better get back home before her parents.

As she passed the Lawtons' house again, she heard shouts of "Traitor!" and a few stones bounced off the closed shutters. Her heart sank.

The next day the Giffords learned that the merchants with tea commissions had held their own private meeting in Mr. Clarke's waterfront warehouse. The Sons of Liberty marched down from the Liberty Tree to the warehouse and demanded, face to face, that the tea agents resign. When the agents refused, the crowd tore off the warehouse door.

"You see?" said William Gifford to his nephew. "That's the way the likes of Harry Cole behave. Law-abiding folk make their voices heard in a lawful way, at Town Meeting." A meeting had been called for Friday at Faneuil Hall.

Sally wished that all the men (and boys) in Boston thought like her father.

For the next week or so, Boston was calmer. Town Meeting voted against "taxation without consent." The Meeting also appointed a committee, which included William Gifford, to go to the tea merchants and demand that they resign their commissions. This time the tea merchants didn't actually refuse, but they stalled and made excuses about customs regulations. Mr. Gifford came home for noonday dinner quite indignant.

"We found Mr. Lawton in his warehouse counting-room," William Gifford reported as he hung up his cloak. "He stood in the doorway with his haughtiest face on. He said" — Mr. Gifford imitated Lawton's stuffy manner — "'I could not possibly consider any such action without knowing the particulars of my situation. Therefore, gentlemen, I beg you to excuse me from further discourse on the subject.'"

"Mr. Lawton ought to have shown more respect," said Mrs. Gifford. "Colonel Hancock led the committee, which represented Town Meeting." As the fact struck her she added, "*You* were chosen to represent Town Meeting! Quite an honor, Mr. Gifford."

William Gifford flushed modestly and shook his head, but Sally knew it *was* quite an honor. Mr. Lawton might not respect her father, but the men of Boston did.

"'Further discourse,'" muttered Ethan, so low that only Sally heard him. "We'll give him further discourse."

On November 17th, a ship from England arrived in Boston Harbor. Jonathan Clarke, one of the tea merchant Richard Clarke's sons, was a passenger. This ship wasn't carrying tea, but it had left England at the same time as the tea ships bound for Boston. So the tea ships would arrive very soon.

That night, a crowd gathered at the Clarkes' house, shouting and throwing rocks. Jonathan Clarke fired a pistol over their heads, which only made the mob angrier, and they smashed several windows before they left.

The next day, John Hancock again led his committee to ask the tea merchants to resign. William Gifford returned from that meeting looking very sober. "Now they're angry that their homes and families are being threatened. It only makes them more stubborn. I can't blame them." He turned to scowl at Ethan. "I trust that *you* would never go along with such a mob."

"No, sir," said Ethan. "It would make more sense to hit Lawton where it hurts, in his moneybags." Sally flinched at the hard edge in his voice. To her, it sounded like Harry Cole speaking.

Felicity Gifford looked alarmed, too. "You sound like that ruffian, the butcher's boy."

Mr. Gifford's scowl deepened, and he told Ethan, "You're not to damage our neighbor's 'moneybags' — his warehouse — either."

But Ethan's idea made an alarming kind of sense, Sally admitted to herself. Mr. Lawton's warehouse on the Long Wharf housed his counting-room, with his ledgers and other business records, as well as his equipment and stored goods. If the Sons of Liberty destroyed Mr. Lawton's warehouse, he wouldn't be able to receive the tea. The trouble was . . . if Mr. Lawton was at the warehouse when they attacked, he might be treated as a "malignant and dangerous person," as the letter in the *Massachusetts Spy* had put it.

"The citizens of Boston will deal with the tea agents in an orderly way," Mr. Gifford finished.

"I'm sure they will, sir," Ethan replied.

Sally thought that answer meant he wouldn't promise anything. William Gifford must have thought so, too, because he leaned across the table to lock eyes with Ethan. "I forbid attacking the warehouse. Forbid it. Do you hear?"

There was a tiny pause, and then Ethan said, "Yes, sir."

Sally let out the breath she was holding. With Ethan out of the plan to attack Mr. Lawton's warehouse, she was free to warn Kitty. Sally didn't mind informing against Harry Cole. The note she would write was already forming in her head:

Dear Kitty,
I am afraid for your Father's safety. You must tell him not to go to his Warehouse this evening. They plan to tear it down!
Your Friend,
Sally

The next morning Sally was awakened before daylight by her father's and stepmother's anxious voices. "Outright defiance!" said Mr. Gifford. "I've been too easy with him, my Sarah's brother's boy."

"You don't know for a fact where he went," said Mrs. Gifford, but she didn't sound as if she believed that.

Sally pushed open her bed curtains. The only light in the kitchen came from the hearth, where her father had re-kindled the fire. Mr. and Mrs. Gifford stood with their arms folded, moving uncertainly from side to side. Josiah pattered out of the bedroom in his nightshirt. "Where's Ethan?" No one answered him.

Sally's stepmother turned to her. "Do you know where Ethan went?"

"No, ma'am," said Sally. She added, "He said he wouldn't go out with Harry's gang." But she remembered with a sinking heart how Ethan had actually answered his uncle. Mr. Gifford had said, "I forbid it . . . Do you hear?"

Ethan had said, "Yes, sir." Meaning, *Yes, I hear*. Not *Yes, I obey*.

12

ETHAN IS MISSING

"But he did go out." William Gifford's forehead knotted with worry. "The question is, why didn't he come back?"

Sally had no answer, but an image flashed in her mind: Mr. Lawton facing a crowd with a pistol in his hand. That was the way the boy Christopher Seider had died.

Mr. Gifford might have seen the same scene in his mind's eye, because he shook his head as if to get something out of it. "Well! It'll do no good to stand here in the middle of the floor."

So Sally went back into her alcove to get dressed, but when she came out, William Gifford was standing in ' middle of the floor again. As Sally started toward the shed, her father called to her. "Sally, leave the cov Run to Uncle Frank's, see if Ethan's been there."

Uncle Frank and Aunt Patience and thei'

near the waterfront on Cow Lane. Sally was glad to help look for Ethan, although it felt strange to be hurrying down Summer Street toward the docks instead of leading Buttercup to pasture. The sun was not up, but the eastern sky was light when Sally reached the Downses' house. Sally hoped that Ethan himself would come to the door, yawning and shamefaced.

Instead, Ethan's mother, a slight woman with a worn but pretty face, appeared with a half-dressed toddler clinging to her skirts. "Why, Sally — come in. What is it, so early? Is the baby ill? Or Felicity?"

When Sally explained that Ethan was missing, an anxious frown creased Aunt Patience's forehead. "We haven't seen him here," she said as she buttoned the little cousin's smock. "Not since last Sunday. We did hear a commotion last night from the direction of Long Wharf. And there's been talk that the Sons of Liberty would send an apprentice gang to one of the tea agents' warehouses."

"Might Uncle Frank know something?" asked Sally. Her uncle would be out fishing, this time of the day.

Aunt Patience shrugged. "Maybe. We'll see, when he brings the boat back in. But he wouldn't have taken Ethan along — especially if the boy was in trouble with William."

Sally wished she hadn't brought worrisome news. Ethan's mother was trying not to sound distressed, but she was twisting her apron strings. The toddler tugged at her mother's skirt and repeated, "Ethan. Ethan."

Aunt Patience spoke again, as if she couldn't help letting

her worries out. "What if word about Lawton's warehouse got to *them*" — she nodded in the direction of the harbor, where the British warships floated — "and they came in last night with a press gang? My own brother was impressed right off the docks here, you know."

Sally did know about that incident, which had happened before Ethan was born. A press gang from a British warship, shorthanded for seamen, had rowed up to the waterfront one day. They'd grabbed a number of young fishermen, including Aunt Patience's older brother, and hauled them back to the ship. Just like that, five Boston men disappeared into the British navy. Ethan's uncle was never heard of again.

"But they don't impress Boston men any more, do they?" asked Sally.

"No, of course not." Aunt Patience took a deep breath. Then she dropped her apron strings and declared, "Listen to me fretting over imaginary troubles! Ethan had no business with that mob, and no business worrying us so. When he does show his face, William ought to give him a good strapping."

Leaving the Downses' house, Sally stood in the lane for a moment. If she were a boy, she'd find out what had happened last night. She'd ask in one of the sailors' inns near Long Wharf. But girls from respectable families didn't venture alone into those inns, even in the morning. Unwillingly she turned to climb back up Summer Street.

Sally hoped that Ethan would be in the house — or in the backyard, getting his strapping from her father — by the time she returned. But at breakfast his chair remained empty.

After the meal Sally took Josiah to Dame Hewes and came back, and still no Ethan.

As Sally was sweeping the shop floor, the bell over the door tinkled. Mr. Gifford and Sally both looked up. Uncle Frank, not Ethan, leaned in the doorway.

"I'll not dirty your floor, William." Frank Downs pointed to his boots, which were crusted with fish scales. He looked very sober, and Sally's heart sank as he went on. "I talked to some of the lads who broke into Lawton's warehouse last night."

"Was Ethan with them?" Sally blurted out.

Her father frowned at her for interrupting, but Uncle Frank nodded. "But they don't know where he is now. There were pistol shots, and shouting — the butcher's boy said he heard British accents — and they ran for it. They all went different ways in the dark."

Pistol shots. Sally flinched and clutched the broom handle as if to defend herself.

William Gifford rose from his bench. "I forbade him to go out," he said heavily as he joined his brother-in-law at the door. "I'd gotten wind of what Harry Cole's gang was up to . . . I didn't think he'd disobey me outright."

Uncle Frank nodded grimly. Then he said, "I hoped Ethan might have been arrested. But none of the magistrates in town have him."

Mr. Gifford pulled off his leather apron, tugged on his coat, and clapped his hat on his head. "Come, Frank. The tide's in. I'll help you search the docks." Over his shoulder he said, "Mind the shop, Sally. Tell your mother where I went."

Sally felt cold and hollow. Her father and uncle were going to search the docks because Ethan might have been shot and then thrown into the harbor. She tried not to imagine his lanky body floating face down under a pier.

Sally wished she could have gone with her father and uncle to search the docks, instead of waiting for news. She finished sweeping the floor and the front steps. She'd polished the brass doorknob just yesterday, but she took a rag and polished it some more, glancing over her shoulder at the traffic on Winter Street. If only, among the stream of peddlers, shoppers, apprentices, men and women of business, wagons, and carriages, Ethan would appear!

"Oys, oys!" The cry of Mr. Hobbes, the oyster-monger, rose above the clamor from the other side of Marlborough Street. Sally remembered that Mrs. Gifford had talked about an oyster stew for dinner. She was about to run to the kitchen for a pail and some money when James Lawton appeared around the corner, heading toward the shoemaker's shop.

Was James on his way to school? But classes must have already begun by this time of morning. Besides, Kitty had written that since his beating, James had stopped going to school.

James halted at the shop door. He glanced at Sally, looked down at the cobblestones, started to turn away, then turned back. He let out a heavy sigh. "Good morning."

"Good morning." Sally couldn't imagine what was wrong with him.

James pushed his hands into his coat pockets, cleared his throat, and looked down at Sally's feet. "He's at Fort William," he muttered. "In the guardhouse."

"What! Who?" Sally's stomach flipped. "Do you mean — ?" As James opened his mouth to speak again, she added, "No, wait!" The oyster-monger was pushing his wheelbarrow past the shop, close enough to overhear. "Good morning, Mr. Hobbes." The wheelbarrow rattled on up the street, and she whispered to James, "How do you know?"

James looked as if it pained him to tell, but he whispered back, "I heard my father talking. He was angry that the soldiers caught only one boy."

"*Soldiers?* Soldiers from Fort William came into Boston?" Mr. Lawton must have secretly arranged for them to protect his warehouse last night.

At James's nod, Sally asked, "How did your father know . . ." All at once she understood. Mr. Lawton had known when the Sons of Liberty would strike at his warehouse because Kitty had warned him. And Kitty had known because Sally had told her. "Oh, no," she moaned.

James had more to say, and he forced the words out: "They'll deliver him to the Royal Navy, my father said. The warships are always shorthanded for crew." He added, "Please don't tell Mr. Gifford."

"Don't — Are you mad?" Sally burst out. "Of course I'll tell my father. British soldiers have no right to grab apprentices and press them into the navy! The whole town will rise up."

"No!" James forgot to whisper, and a man riding by on horseback looked over curiously. James lowered his voice again. "They'll burn our house down. They'll tar and feather Father."

James was right. And besides, Sally thought miserably, she'd rather not tell whose fault it was. Because it was *her* fault that Ethan was locked up at Fort William, soon to be forced into the Royal Navy. She imagined confessing this to her father and stepmother, or to Uncle Frank and Aunt Patience. That would be even worse — much worse — than the worst moment in her life so far, the night she was caught wearing Kitty's gold ring.

But Ethan! "I have to tell," said Sally. "I'm sorry, James. As soon as I say where Ethan is, they'll know right away that Mr. Lawton called the soldiers in." Her voice trembled. "Ethan *must* be rescued before — And I can't rescue him myself!"

James shook his head in distress. "Don't tell, I beg you. There must be another way. Give me some time to think."

Sally felt torn in two directions. James had trusted her with this precious information, although he was afraid for his family. But *she* was sick with fear for Ethan! Could there be another way to help him, besides telling Father?

"Listen," Sally blurted out, "I won't tell right away. I'll give you enough time to warn your father that the Sons of Liberty found out what he did to Ethan. And enough time for all of you to flee to the governor's in Milton. I'll wait until — dawn tomorrow."

James looked uncertain. As he opened his mouth to answer, a man crossed the street to the shoemaker's shop. It was Mr. Ward, the tailor. "I thought I'd walk to Town Meeting with Mr. Gifford," he said to Sally. "Unless he's left already."

Town Meeting again today. Sally explained to Mr. Ward that her father was out looking for her cousin, and she didn't know if he'd get to the meeting.

"Well, well! I'm sorry to hear that," said the tailor. Starting to walk on, he focused on James. "I'll wager *his* father won't dare show his face at Town Meeting."

James gave Sally a look as if to say, *You see? They all hate us.* Before turning away, he put his finger across his lips.

Sally nodded. She was already sorry for it, but she'd promised silence — until dawn.

As James disappeared around the corner again, further questions rose in Sally's mind: Since James was so worried about his family's safety, why had he revealed this dangerous information to Sally?

More disturbing, there were all the questions about Kitty. Had Kitty known that her father summoned soldiers from the fort to protect his warehouse? Had Kitty known that Ethan was captured? Why hadn't Kitty, instead of James, informed Sally? Didn't Kitty care what would happen to Ethan? She'd called him "uncouth," and maybe he was — but he was Sally's kin. Sally felt betrayed.

Hannah had warned her that she couldn't trust Kitty, the wealthy tea merchant's daughter. But Sally herself was the real traitor.

William Gifford returned late, and Felicity Gifford waited the noonday dinner for him. Mr. Gifford hadn't, of course, found Ethan's body in the harbor. He and Uncle Frank had asked at all the warehouses, and all the taverns near the waterfront, and talked to the night watchmen in that neighborhood, searching for some hint of what had happened to Ethan.

As a last resort, they'd gone to Edmund Lawton's house. "First he wouldn't see Frank and me," William Gifford reported. "Then he came to the door and said he'd talk to us after we'd repaired the damage to his warehouse. Finally he admitted he'd fired his pistol, but he said he aimed it into the air, to scare the gang, and they ran 'like the cowards they were.' He said it wasn't his affair what happened to any of them after that."

Sally imagined Mr. Lawton looking down his nose at her worried father and uncle, saying it "wasn't his affair," when he knew exactly what had happened to Ethan. She was so angry, she almost blurted out what she knew.

Before Sally could speak, Felicity Gifford said in a hard voice, "No, why should Edmund Lawton care what became of a shoemaker's apprentice?" There was a pause, and then she asked her husband, "Will you go to Town Meeting this afternoon?"

Mr. Gifford shook his head. "I haven't the heart for it. I'd best be at home, in case we get word about the boy." His eye fell on Sally. "Come to the shop with me, Sally. I've a stack of notes to be written."

In the shop, William Gifford got out his ledger book and showed Sally the accounts due. She began writing bills, while he sat down at his workbench and slid a shoe onto a last. For a while they both worked without speaking, to the sounds of Mr. Gifford's hammer tapping and Sally's pen scratching. Now and then Sally's father gave a deep sigh.

Sally wished she could assure him that Ethan was alive, at least. She shouldn't have promised James to wait until tomorrow. Maybe the Lawtons were already in their carriage by now, headed for Milton. "Father," she said.

William Gifford looked up from his work, raising his eyebrows. Sally gulped and hesitated. Just then, the shop bell jingled.

Sally's father lifted a hand for her to wait. "Good afternoon, Master Lawton," he said.

James! Sally's head swiveled toward the door. "What are you doing here?" she exclaimed. He ought to be at home, packing, or on his way to Milton with the rest of the family.

Sally's father gave her a puzzled frown, but James paid no attention. He walked into the shop with a limp, holding up a shoe heel. "Sir, can this be mended?" He took off one buckled shoe, showing the heel missing.

"Certainly, if you like to wait." Mr. Gifford took the shoe and heel and examined them. "Hmm. Didn't I make these very shoes for you, only this summer? How did the heel come off so soon?" He squinted at the bottom of the shoe, then the heel, and back again. "Why, you could hardly *pry* the heel off with a chisel."

James, taking a seat in a chair by the door, looked pleased with himself. He had pried the heel off; Sally felt sure of it. So the heel was an excuse to come into the shop.

Murmuring about needing an old broadside for blotting paper, Sally crossed the shop to the waiting area. James looked up eagerly and put his hand in his coat pocket.

Hoping that Mr. Gifford's head was bent over his work, Sally managed to place herself in front of the bench so that her father's view of James was blocked. She mouthed, *Did you tell your father? Are you leaving town now?*

James mouthed something back, but Sally couldn't make out the words. Was he saying "Milton"? Something beginning with "M," at least. And "Kitty"? Maybe — it was a "K" or "C" word, anyway. Oh, dear. Sally leaned forward to pick up a broadside, hoping James would take the chance to whisper. Instead, he gave her a folded paper.

"Sally," said Mr. Gifford.

Sally whirled around, holding the note hidden behind the broadside. But her father only said, "If you're finished with the bills, you'd better go help your mother with supper."

Nodding obediently, Sally tried to hide her excitement. Of course the note was from Kitty, and it would explain everything. How thoughtful of Kitty to write Sally, and how good of James to bring her the note, in the midst of the Lawtons' scramble to get out of Boston!

There was no private place between the workshop and the kitchen to read the note, although Sally managed to slip it into her pocket. It was hard to leave it there unread, even for a little while.

In the kitchen, Mrs. Gifford looked up from the butter churn. "Sally, see if you can find four good-size parsnips for the stew." She nodded toward the backyard.

Eagerly Sally hurried outside and knelt in the vegetable garden with her back to the house. She took out the note and unfolded the paper.

That was not Kitty's loopy handwriting, but a precise, tight script. Sally's eyes jumped to the bottom of the densely written page, to the signature: *James*.

Her baffled gaze flicked back to the top. *Meet me at Midnight*, the note began.

Sally put a hand over her mouth in dismay. What kind of harebrained scheme was this?

13

MEET ME AT MIDNIGHT

James's note went on to explain his plan. The details, what there were of them, dismayed Sally even further: He and Sally would sneak down to the waterfront, where the skiff to the Lawtons' barge was tied. They would row the skiff out to Castle Island and climb up to the fort.

Sally and James, row across the harbor on a dark November night? To Fort William? Sally pictured the fort as it had appeared through James's spyglass last summer. Only now she imagined its hulking stone walls looming forward as if to crush her.

Even if Sally and James managed to steal the skiff in the first place (there would certainly be a night watchman at the dock, wouldn't there?) and reach Castle Island (what if the water was rough?), how would they get into the fort? Sally remembered the massive gate at the top of the bluff, and the red-coated soldiers standing guard, muskets on their shoulders. On that day in August the British soldiers had saluted Mr. Lawton and welcomed his party — but they wouldn't be quite so welcoming to a couple of sneaks in the middle of the night.

James's note skipped over all these obstacles to explain what they would do inside the fort. While Sally waited near the guardhouse for a chance to free Ethan, James would set off an explosion.

An explosion! Sally remembered how she and Kitty had laughed over James's blackened face, the result of an experiment with explosives, last spring. It didn't seem funny now.

James would ignite his explosives, the plan went on, near the munitions, the gunpowder stores, which luckily were in a bastion on the opposite side of the fort from the guardhouse. Here he'd drawn a tidy little map of Fort William. The guardhouse and the gunpowder stores, as well as the sentry posts, were carefully labeled. The British troops would be alarmed, thinking their munitions were blowing up, and they'd all run toward the noise.

While the guardhouse sentry and the rest of the garrison headed for the munitions, James's plan continued, Sally would take the keys from the peg, unlock the guardhouse, and free Ethan from his cell. James would meet Sally and Ethan down at the docks, and they'd row back to Boston.

Was James stark raving mad? Just the thought of scrambling through the fort, with musket balls whistling toward her back, made Sally cringe. Even if she did manage to free

Ethan from the guardhouse, the three of them would never make it back to the boat.

Shoving the note into her pocket, Sally began yanking parsnips. What a witless idea, and what a waste of time! Why hadn't James just done as Sally told him and got Mr. Lawton to hustle his family out of Boston?

Back in the kitchen, Sally fumed and worried as she trimmed and scrubbed and chopped the vegetables. She should tell her father where Ethan was, right now. He'd rouse the town, and the people of Boston would force the governor to get Ethan back from Castle Island.

But surely as soon as the town was roused, a mob would descend on the Lawtons' house. Sally was very angry with Kitty, and she thought it would serve her right to be frightened, but she didn't want her — or James — to be hurt. This time, Sally feared, the mob wouldn't stop at breaking a few windows.

Supper went by, the evening chores were done, and bedtime came. Maybe, Sally thought, it was best for her to do nothing. When she didn't meet James at midnight, he'd realize that his plan for rescuing Ethan was a bad one, wouldn't he? Wouldn't he go back home and wake up his father and sister? Then, finally, the Lawtons would flee from Boston. She must give them time to get away.

Crawling under her quilt, Sally stared into the dark. The trouble was, she didn't know what James would or wouldn't realize. His mind worked in unpredictable ways. If she didn't meet him, maybe he'd come to the Giffords' and try to wake her up. Or maybe he'd try to rescue Ethan by himself.

Should she tell Father, after all? Sally's mind went around and around, like a leg of mutton on a spit, without getting anywhere. She was sure she'd lie awake all night.

Sally awoke in the dark as the night watchman called out from Common Street: "Twelve o' the clock and all's well." She recognized that reedy voice; evidently Mr. Ward was on duty again tonight. "Calm skies with scanty clouds. Waxing moon, about to set."

The contents of Sally's mind seemed to have sorted themselves out in her sleep. It now seemed perfectly clear what she must do. Moving quickly and silently, she tiptoed into the kitchen and found a pair of Ethan's outgrown breeches and coat in the chest. She put on her own shift instead of a shirt; no one would see it under the coat. And there was nothing particularly girlish about her cloak.

Dressed, Sally pulled her hair back and tied it at the nape of her neck, as boys did. At the back door she quietly lifted the bar and closed the door behind her. She wished she didn't have to leave her family's door unbarred in the middle of the night.

Even as Sally tiptoed past the cowshed, she could hardly believe what she was doing. Last summer she'd floated to Castle Island in a pink flounced dress. Just this morning, she'd hesitated to venture into the rough waterfront neighborhood to ask about Ethan. And yet tonight she was sneaking off in boys' clothes to raid the fort.

The half-full moon was low over the bare trees on the Common, but it gave enough light to show James waiting for her at the well. He started as she stepped through the hedge. "Who — Sally?"

"It's me," she said, glad that her disguise seemed to be working.

James nodded and took a deep breath. "I've got the powder and a flint and steel," he said, pointing his chin at a pouch slung over his shoulder. "And a fuse."

Sally's stomach tightened at the mention of explosives, but she only said, "Let's go, then." She beckoned James to follow her down the alley.

Winter Street seemed deserted, although here and there a dog heard their footsteps and barked. But just as Sally and James reached Marlborough Street, a voice behind them rapped out, "Who's there?" It was Mr. Ward, tonight's watchman. Holding up his lantern with one hand and a cudgel with the other, he peered at them through the gloom. In a milder tone he added, "Is that — Ethan Downs?"

Sally froze. James started to answer: "No, we're — ow!" Sally had stepped hard on his foot. They were in the shadows, but Mr. Ward might recognize James's voice. He might recognize *hers*.

"No, sir." She made her voice hoarse and turned away from Mr. Ward. "We — we're going to fetch the midwife for mother. We need to make haste — goodnight, sir."

"Ah, the midwife." The tailor still sounded puzzled, but he added, "Godspeed, then."

Sally's heart seemed to pound in her throat as she and James hurried across Marlborough Street. Did she look like Ethan? Maybe a bit, wearing his clothes, in the dark.

James whispered, "Midwife! Good thinking."

Sally flushed with pride, but she hardly had time to be pleased with herself. She'd just spotted another night watchman in the direction of the Liberty Tree, and he was turning their way. "Hurry," she gasped.

Closer to the waterfront, there were a few more people on the streets, mostly men. The other night wanderers made Sally feel that she and James were less noticeable. On the other hand, anybody still out and about at midnight was probably up to no good.

As Sally and James were making their way down Water Street, the door of a tavern burst open. A party of sailors poured out, laughing and cursing. Before Sally and James could dart away, one of the sailors stumbled toward them. "See here, fellows," he called to his mates over his shoulder. "Two likely lads for cabin boys." His words puffed out on fumes of rum, and he reached for Sally.

Sally tried to duck, slipped on the damp cobblestones, and almost fell, but James grabbed her arm and yanked her away. "More 'likely' a knife in your ribs, wharf rat!" he snarled. The sailors shouted insults back, but they were too drunk to give chase.

Sally and James hurried onward. Sally kept glancing at her companion — James certainly was full of surprises! He'd launched this risky adventure to rescue the lad his own father had sent to the guardhouse. And just now, he'd sounded as mean as Harry Cole. "Do you really have a knife?" she whispered.

"Well — a penknife." James laughed shakily. "We didn't wish to become cabin boys, did we?"

Around another corner, they heard masts creaking, and waves lapping the piers. They had reached the waterfront — near a distillery, to judge by the smell of fermenting molasses. Here and there the shadowy forms of warehouses and ships were smudged with light from watchmen's lanterns.

Among the ships anchored beyond the wharves, Sally picked out the silhouette of the British warship *Captain*. What if Ethan had already been turned over to the navy? She would not think about that. "At least it's a calm night," she said.

"Yes, lucky for us," said James, "and the tide's coming in. We can row across Dorchester Flats instead of going around by the deep channel."

If we get away with the boat, thought Sally.

James paused to survey the waterfront. "There." He pointed to a nearby dock. "That's our skiff."

Sally followed James onto the dock. "You put the oars in," she whispered. "I'll cast off."

Setting the lantern down, Sally knelt on the rough boards of the dock and began to unwind the rope from the cleat. If only the oarlocks didn't clatter so loudly!

Without warning, a light jumped out from the shadows of the distillery. Footsteps slapped the cobblestones and clumped onto the dock. "Who's there?" a rough voice called out.

Sally gasped. She freed the last loop of the rope and jumped down into the boat.

"Stop!" shouted the watchman. He lunged toward them.

Dropping onto the bench, Sally grabbed an oar and pushed off from the dock. "Row!"

Sally and James struggled away from the dock, digging their oars into the water and jerking the skiff this way and that. They muttered frantic instructions to each other without listening. They bumped into other small craft. At one point, they spun the skiff all the way around.

Sally was afraid the watchman would jump in another boat and come after them, but he only shouted at them from the end of the dock. "Stop, I say! I'll sound the alarm!"

Then Sally had the idea to count time, like a coxswain, as she pulled on her oar. "One . . . two," she gasped. "*Pull . . . two . . . one . . . two.*" James fell into her rhythm, and finally they began to make progress. It was progress in zigzags, but at least the distance from the dock widened, and the watchman's light dwindled.

Sally's heartbeat slowed down, and she realized that the muscles in her arms were trembling. "Don't row so hard," she begged James. "I can't keep up."

James pulled more gently, and the skiff straightened itself. They threaded their way around the bulky shapes of merchant ships. Uncle Frank would be taking his fishing boat out in a few hours, thought Sally, when the tide turned.

Last summer, when Sally dressed in Kitty's fine clothes for the trip to Castle Island, Uncle Frank hadn't recognized her. Would he recognize her if he saw her dressed like a boy? Mr. Ward, the tailor, had wondered if she was Ethan! It was so strange that clothes — "mere clothes," as the pastor said when he preached against vanity — could make people think she was someone else.

When Sally and James were clear of the moored ships, James pointed out the brightest star in the eastern sky. "The Dog Star. That's the direction of Castle Island." They plied their oars in silence for a while, glancing over their shoulders to keep on course. Now that they were away from lanterns and torches, the sky seemed light compared with the black shore. So did the water, reflecting the sky.

Sally seemed to be in an eerie dream, with a strange — although likeable — companion. There was so much she didn't understand about James. The strangest thing was that he'd cooked up this risky scheme to save the boy who'd attacked his father's warehouse.

"James," she said finally, "Why do you want to rescue Ethan? He isn't *your* cousin. In fact, your family and our family are . . . enemies."

James stopped rowing to turn toward her. "Why do I — ?" He sounded surprised that she didn't understand. "It's a point of honor."

"Honor?" That word came up a lot in the thrilling novels Kitty read, but Sally wouldn't have expected it from James.

"I tried to explain it to my father," said James. "Ethan stood up to Harry Cole for me, that time down at the docks last summer. But my father wouldn't listen — he was determined to punish one fellow from the mob, at least."

"Ethan told me he tried to shield you from the tar." Sally spoke slowly, searching her memory for what Ethan had actually said.

"He did a great deal more than that," said James. "He knocked the tar brush out of Harry's hand, and he punched the lad holding me — punched him in the stomach — and he shouted at me, 'Run, you stupid mooncalf!' It was only because of him that I didn't come home with blisters all over, instead of just on my neck."

"I didn't know that Ethan *rescued* you from the gang," said Sally. Ethan might have told her everything that happened, she realized now, if she hadn't accused him at the outset and made him angry at her. A further thought struck Sally, and she asked James urgently, "Did Kitty know?"

"Kitty? No — why would I tell my sister? I don't tell her anything, if I can help it."

So that was a relief, at least, thought Sally. Kitty had not known that the boy her father sent to the fort was her brother's savior.

By this time they could make out their goal, Castle Island, a distinctive black bulge between the sea and sky. Amber dots glowed from sentry lights on the fort. And in that fort, Sally thought, waited hundreds of British soldiers with muskets and bayonets. In the skiff crouched two foolhardy children.

As the skiff drew closer to Castle Island, Sally saw a thread of white foam marking the water's edge. She thought she also glimpsed a flicker of light where the landing must be. "Sentries!" she whispered. "We forgot about sentries at the quay. We'll have to land somewhere else."

James cast a glance over his shoulder. "I don't see any light," he said. "Your eyes must be playing tricks on you. Weren't you paying attention, when we toured the fort last summer? They don't post a watch at the quay."

Sally remembered James asking Lieutenant Burton dozens of questions, but she didn't remember all the answers. Craning her neck again, she strained to see through the dark. The light on the shore, if there had been a light, was gone. "Still," she said, "let's not tie up at the quay."

"That'll be easier, anyway," James agreed. "We can just pull up on the beach."

They drew closer and closer, until the bluff loomed overhead and they could hear ripples sloshing the shore. When the bottom of the skiff scraped on pebbles, Sally and James shipped the oars and clambered out into the icy knee-deep water. "One — two — three!" Together they slid and bumped the boat out of the water.

"Farther up," panted James. "Or else it'll float out with the tide."

"But it makes such a racket!" Sally was afraid that even the sentries on the fort walls, high above, could have heard them drag the skiff.

"Come on!" James began to count again. "One — two — "

"And three!" As the deep voice broke in, a sudden light shone in their eyes. Only a few yards away, a soldier held up a lantern. Sally and James blinked in the yellow glow.

14

FORT WILLIAM

"Halt in the King's name!" barked a second man's voice.

"Aye," growled the first man, "halt or we shoot."

"We're halting!" gasped Sally. She glanced at James. He looked dumbfounded.

The soldier with the lantern stepped forward. "Why, it's only a pair of lads, Ned."

The second soldier, Ned, also stepped forward to peer at Sally and James. Sally stared back at him — there was something familiar about that face with the long chin and broken nose.

"Aye," said Ned, resting the butt of his musket on the ground, "a pair of lads. Now, what might they be doing here?" He squinted at James, and at the pouch over James's shoulder. "And what might they be carrying in that fat bag?"

The gunpowder! If they found it —

"To tell the truth, sir," quavered James, "we're visiting a prisoner. Our cousin." He patted the pouch. "We're bringing him some — cheese and a jug of cider."

Sally doubted that flimsy story would keep the sentries from searching James's pouch, but in desperation she chimed in. "Oh, sir! They're going to send our cousin off to the navy, and he'll never see home again." She forced a sob. "You wouldn't begrudge him a little last comfort, would you?"

The soldier named Ned smiled — not a very nice smile — and rubbed his long chin. "Such a sad story . . . but I don't see how we could go against regulations, do you, Simon?"

"Go against regulations?" The soldier with the lantern frowned a little, as if he wasn't sure what Ned was up to. "I should say not!"

Ned shook his head sorrowfully, but he made no move to either arrest James and Sally or force them to leave the island. He seemed, in fact, to be settling down for a chat. "Let's take a look at their craft, Simon." Motioning the other man to bring the lantern closer, he put a hand on the Lawtons' skiff. "Now, isn't this a tidy little boat. Mm-hm. Just the thing for slipping across the harbor on a calm evening."

James's eyes darted from Sally to Ned as if he had an idea. "It might be of interest to you gentlemen," he said in a firmer voice, "that we also brought a certain amount of silver. I thought it might help smooth our cousin's way in the King's Navy. But now I see that if you kind gentlemen let us pass, you would deserve a reward."

Sally saw what James was getting at, and she felt a spark

of hope. These men did not sound like trustworthy sentries, but for that very reason she and James might be able to make a bargain with them. "Oh, please, sirs. I can see by your faces that you have tender feelings. If only you saw our cousin's dear mother weep for him, it would wring your heart, sir."

A look passed between the two sentries. Simon was still frowning, but he gave a little shrug. Ned smiled more broadly at Sally, then at James, who had pulled a small silk bag from his coat pocket. "Of course it would. *We* have dear mothers who would weep for us, don't we, Simon?"

James opened the drawstring of his bag and started to count out coins, but Ned held out his hand, palm up and fingers wiggling. "No, no. The whole purse, if you don't mind."

"But sir," begged Sally with a sudden thought, "we'll need a gift for the sentries up there, too." She nodded toward the top of the bluff.

"Ah," said Ned. "I take your meaning. But we'll let you in on a secret." He winked at his fellow sentry. "The wicket door in the gate isn't barred! You see, we have a little arrangement with our friend up there. At the end of our shift, we might find him cat-napping. With the door unbarred, no need to disturb him." He nodded reassuringly from Sally to James. "As long as you're quiet, see, you can slip through the gate like weasels through a rat hole."

The soldier called Simon gave a harsh laugh. "Aye — like eels into a pie."

Sally didn't like the way they were talking, and James seemed uneasy, too. But what else could they do? If the sentries wanted to, they could take the money *and* James's pouch, *and* hand Sally and James over as spies.

James must have been thinking along the same lines, because he dropped the silk purse into Ned's hand and nodded to Sally.

"Quiet, now!" advised Ned in a friendly tone as Sally and James started toward the bluff.

They slipped and stumbled over the pebbles as their eyes got used to the dark again. Sally glanced back twice, suspicious that the sentries might signal someone up on the fort. But the two British soldiers were only standing beside the skiff, Ned patting the bow and talking in a low, rapid voice.

Reaching the stone stairway from the beach to the fort, Sally and James began to climb. "You said there wouldn't be any sentries at the landing!" hissed Sally. She was indignant that James had made such a mistake, and annoyed with herself for taking his word for it.

"There shouldn't have been any!" answered James. His voice shook, as if he was imagining how narrowly they'd missed being shot. "There weren't any sentries last summer. Lieutenant Burton told me they didn't bother, because the bluffs are enough protection."

"Never mind," said Sally. They both should have known the fort would be on the alert now, with all the unrest in town. She gazed up toward the next obstacle, the gate at the top of the stairway. "Now we have to — " At a noise down on the beach, Sally stopped with one foot on the next step.

James also stopped short. "What's that?" It was the noise

of something heavy, bumping over the pebbles.

They peered down through the gloom to the water's edge. A light bobbed beyond the foam at the shore, then vanished as if someone had thrown a blanket over a lantern. "They're taking our boat!" exclaimed James.

"No!" Sally couldn't believe it. "Why would — Oh." All the puzzling little signs she'd noticed at the time, but brushed aside, came back to her now. "They're deserting!" That was the only reason the sentries had let them go.

"Deserting — yes, that's it." James blew out his breath in disgust. "I did wonder why they were pretending to be so kind." He added, "They're the 'weasels.'"

"But we're the 'eels in a pie,'" said Sally bitterly. "How can we save Ethan if we don't even have a boat?"

That stopped James for a moment. Then he said, "We'll just have to take a boat from the quay. Never mind that now — let's go."

They climbed on up the stone staircase; it was the only thing to do. As they drew closer to the gate, Sally could see the wicket door, outlined by flickering torchlight inside. An unpleasant thought struck Sally: had the sentries lied about the wicket door being unbarred?

They paused on the last step. As Sally reached out to try the door, measured footsteps thumped the pavement on the other side. James silently seized her arm, but Sally was already shrinking back. The sentry at the gate was not catnapping.

Sally held her breath, heart thudding. The sentry's

footsteps faded.

Sally reached out again and pushed the door. It swung inward with a squeal. James gasped and grabbed the door. Sally was sure the sentry must have heard the noise, and she tensed to flee.

But after listening for a moment, James edged through the opening. He beckoned to Sally, and she followed.

Crossing the lighted space, James led the way along the parapet. He stopped short of a bastion lit by another torch and guarded by another sentry. James and Sally crouched behind a barrel, watching the sentry pace in and out of the light.

"The guardhouse," mouthed James. He pointed to the iron-bound door, then to the ring with two keys hanging beside the door.

Sally nodded. She didn't want James to leave her here alone. At the same time, she desperately wanted to get on with it. "Why don't you go?" she whispered. She could hear James's shallow breathing. "What's the matter?"

"I am going," said James. He adjusted the strap of the pouch on his shoulder, but for a moment longer he didn't move. Finally he half-rose, tiptoed into the shadows, and disappeared.

Sally pressed her back against the stone wall. Rowing across the harbor had warmed her up, but now the damp cold seeped into her bones, especially her feet, wet from beaching the boat. She clenched her teeth to keep them from chattering. It must be nearly a frost tonight.

The sentry was cold, too, judging from the way he stamped his feet and rubbed his arms. Sally wished she could do the same, but she didn't dare move.

How long would it take James to reach the munitions stores and light a fuse? She hoped he could see what he was doing. She hoped the British sentries *couldn't* see what he was doing. What if they caught James?

Or — what if James managed the explosion, but blew himself up? Terrible accidents could happen with gunpowder. Sally thought of Tom Greene's missing fingertip.

The sentry yawned. He stepped away from the torchlight and scanned the sky. He must be checking the position of the stars, to see how much of his watch had passed.

Sally's thoughts turned back to the two deserters. A question occurred to her: Why had Ned and Simon stolen James's skiff? Of course they needed a boat in order to desert, but why hadn't they taken one of the fort's boats tied up at the quay?

Unless there weren't any boats at the quay. Sally and James hadn't actually seen boats there; it was too dark. James had been wrong about the sentries, and he could be wrong about the boats.

That idea was too awful to think about for very long. Sally turned her thoughts toward where the runaway soldiers would go, once they crossed the harbor. Would they head for the countryside? According to what she'd overheard from the workers at the Greenes' farm, at least one deserter had turned up in Concord.

But Sally doubted whether a sly fellow like Ned would want to work on a farm as a hired hand. Besides, two British soldiers would have a better chance of losing themselves in Boston's crowded waterfront. Strangers from all over the world were always coming and going down at the wharves.

How many of the soldiers in the regiment at Fort William would desert, if they got a chance? During Sally's visit to the fort with Kitty this summer, she'd been dazzled by the officers, especially Lieutenant Burton. She hadn't paid much attention to the ordinary soldiers. The only individual she'd remembered was the sentry at the gate with the greasy jacket.

Boom. From the other side of the fort, a thunder so deep that the stones trembled. Sally jerked away from the wall, her heart racing again. In the distance there were shouts, running footsteps.

Clutching his musket, the sentry called out, "What is it?"

Go, Sally silently urged the sentry. Why didn't he run to see what was happening? That was the plan! She glanced at the ring of keys on the peg, then quickly away, as if her attention could remind the soldier to guard the prisoners. If he stayed at his post, James's plan was ruined.

The moments dragged on. The soldier shifted his weight from foot to foot and peered into the dark. What if he left *and* took the keys with him?

An alarm bell clanged out on the parade ground, and the noise seemed to make up the sentry's mind. Musket at the ready, he plunged toward the uproar.

Almost before the sentry disappeared, Sally dashed out of the shadows and seized the iron keys. The large one must fit the outer door? Sure enough, it slid into the lock. She swung the heavy door open.

"Ethan?" Sally called into the dark space.

"Who's there?" demanded a hoarse voice. Another man's voice said wonderingly, "It's a young lad, come to rescue us." A third man growled, "Shut your mouth, you fool. You're dreaming."

"Ethan!" Sally repeated. "Where are you?"

"Sally? Sally!" Finally, Ethan's voice over the rising babble. "Here! Is that really you? I'm here, at the end!"

Scurrying down the dim corridor, Sally felt for the edge of his door and the lock. Ethan babbled at her through the clamor from the other prisoners. "What in the name of heaven — ? How did you — ?" He clutched at her arm through the bars. Disturbingly, Sally thought she heard him sob.

"Hush!" she hissed. "Leave me be!" She found the keyhole and pushed the smaller key in. It stuck, grated — and finally turned.

The cell door clanged open. "Thank God!" groaned Ethan. Sally grabbed his hand and pulled him toward the guardhouse door. Someone breathing hoarsely squeezed past her, shoving her off balance, and her jacket caught on a prong of hardware. At first she thought Ethan had jostled her, but the silhouette in the guardhouse doorway was short and stocky.

"Let *me* out!" shouted another prisoner, and the rest clamored, "Let us out, in the name of mercy!" Sally yanked her jacket free, dropped the keys into the nearest cell, and pressed forward.

Out on the bastion, Ethan blinked at the flickering torchlight. Sally scanned his face anxiously. His right eye was swollen, and he looked as stunned as a mackerel in the fish market.

"This way," she urged, jerking her head. He followed her along the parapet. Their footsteps clattered on the flagstones, but the noise couldn't be helped. Behind them more footsteps sounded, going in the opposite direction. The prisoners must be headed for another exit.

As Sally and Ethan pelted toward the gate, a shout rang across the parade ground: "Halt, or I fire!" Sally saw the well-lit wicket door ahead and thought, *What a fine target we'll make.*

A musket fired, and a musket ball whistled past Sally's ear. Instinctively she dropped to the ground, but Ethan hauled her up. "Go!" He yanked her forward and shoved her through the door. Just as he slammed the door behind them, more musket balls thunked into the wood.

15

THE RESCUE

"Go!" panted Ethan again, nudging Sally. They slipped and stumbled their way down the damp steps. At least, Sally thought gratefully, her cousin had snapped out of his daze.

Down, down, down the stairway to the beach. From up on the fort, they heard shouts: "Halt!" "Fire!" Shots rang out at random, a few striking the stone steps but most bouncing off the pebbles below.

As they scrambled across the beach, Sally flinched with the blast of each shot. The soldiers on the parapet might not be able to see them, but if they peppered the beach with enough musket balls, some were sure to hit Sally and Ethan.

The musket fire stopped abruptly. For an instant Sally was relieved, and then she feared what it might mean. Were the soldiers following them down the stairway?

"Where's your boat?" panted Ethan.

"At the quay," gasped Sally.

"The quay!" Ethan sounded as if the quay was the worst place on the shore to leave her boat.

Of course Sally knew that, but — "Never mind that now!" She grabbed Ethan's arm and jerked him forward toward the quay, barely outlined against the lighter water.

There was at least one boat tied up at the quay, Sally noted as they neared the dock. But it looked enormous, the size of a six-man whaleboat. And where was James? A moan of despair escaped her throat.

"Here!" James's voice, low and urgent, from the other side of the quay. "I'm over here." They followed the sound to where he knelt on the stone dock, struggling with something. "Can't — untie — this — blasted — knot — "

Ethan groaned. "And those scoundrels took my knife."

"James, *you* have a knife!" Sally almost screamed.

"Give it here," snapped Ethan. There was fumbling in the dark. "A *pen*knife?" he exclaimed with disgust. But he went to work with a brisk sawing noise, and something gave way. "Ah!" Ethan exclaimed. "Get in."

They clambered aboard. This boat was smaller than the one Sally had seen first, but larger than the Lawtons' skiff, and there were two pair of oars. Sally and James each took an oar in the stern, while Ethan grabbed the oars in the bow.

"Keep down!" Ethan ordered as they started to row.

"I'm afraid it's impossible to keep down and row at the same time," panted James over his shoulder.

"Don't argue!" begged Sally, although she agreed with

James.

The three of them dug their oars into the water, but the boat hardly moved. Waves slapped it back against the dock. This boat was made to be rowed by four strong men, not a boy and a girl and a youth. No wonder the deserting sentries had stolen the little skiff, thought Sally.

"All together, now." Ethan's voice, with a do-or-die tone that Sally had never heard before, seemed to give her fresh strength. "And . . . *pull* . . . and *pull* . . . and *pull* . . ." He was chanting the beat for them, as Sally had when she and James escaped with the skiff. Slowly but surely, puffing and grunting, they inched away from the dock.

For several minutes the only sounds were splashes, the creaking of the oarlocks, and labored breathing. Then Ethan gasped, "Rest a bit. They aren't giving chase."

Looking up, Sally strained her eyes into the dark between their boat and the edge of Castle Island. No ripple of a wake to show a boat coming after them. She let out a long, shuddering sigh.

James, panting, replied to Ethan, "And the tide's with us now." Then he asked, "Why aren't they chasing us?"

A good question. For a moment Sally couldn't imagine why. Then she remembered the man shoving past her as she and Ethan ran from the guardhouse. "Maybe they're chasing the other prisoners."

"Aye," agreed Ethan. "The fort was all in an uproar. Prisoners running around in the dark, and that explosion — "

"Ahem." James cleared his throat proudly. "The powder

153

did go off just the way I planned."

"That plan of yours!" exclaimed Sally. "I thought you'd taken leave of your wits."

"*James Lawton.*" Ethan sounded suddenly thunderstruck. "Is that really James Lawton in front of me? Son of Edmund Lawton, the Tory tea merchant?"

"Of course it's James," said Sally, swinging around to face her cousin. "No one else could have thought up such an outlandish scheme to rescue you."

Ethan started to speak, but for several moments he could only shake his head and sigh. "Now I know I'm dreaming. Rescued from Fort William by Cousin Sally and Edmund Lawton's son? It's not possible!"

"It was difficult, but not impossible," James corrected him. He shifted in his seat to speak to Ethan. "I knew the layout of the fort, and I'd handled explosives before."

James launched into a description of how he'd managed to "handle" gunpowder next to the fort's munitions store. Sally shuddered to imagine that scene, even though it had turned out well.

Leaning forward, Ethan interrupted James in a low, serious voice. "James Lawton! I am in your debt forever." He added, curiously, "Have you deserted the Tories, then, and joined the Whigs?"

"No," said James. "We Lawtons are Tories. But I was in *your* debt. It was a matter of honor."

"Well!" Ethan started to laugh. "Aren't you the noble young Tory!"

"And aren't you the noble young Son of Liberty!" James retorted. He began laughing, too, and Sally joined in, until they were all laughing themselves silly with relief.

By the time they rowed into the harbor, however, no one was laughing. With weary sighs and grunts the three young people pulled up to a deserted dock and crawled ashore. They trudged silently uphill through the dark streets, keeping their distance from the lanterns of neighborhood watchmen.

As Sally and the boys plodded down the alley behind the Giffords' yard, Sally's mind felt as numb as her toes. Her one thought was of her warm bed waiting inside, and she hardly noticed when James disappeared through the hedge. She crossed the backyard to the kitchen door and lifted the latch — but the door would not open.

At first Sally thought it was only stuck, but as Ethan pushed it with all his might, it became clear that the bar was firmly in place. Sally guessed Father must have gotten up after she left, checked the back door, and fastened the bar again. Had he noticed that Sally was missing?

"We'll have to wake them up," whispered Sally through numb lips. She was trembling with the cold.

"I suppose." Ethan raised his fist to knock on the door, but then he paused at the sound of footsteps inside.

"Who's there?" demanded William Gifford.

"Father, it's Ethan!" Sally managed a sort of mumbled shout.

The door flew open as fast as Mr. Gifford could unbar

it. Holding up a candle, he stared at Ethan. "Thanks be to God," he breathed. He touched his nephew's face near his black eye. In a sterner voice he exclaimed, "Where have you been?"

"Ethan!" Felicity Gifford appeared at the edge of the candlelight. "Am I dreaming?" She seized his hand with both of hers, and her eyes shone with tears. "Where *were* you?" Josiah pattered out of the bedroom and threw himself at Ethan's legs.

They all talked at once: Ethan begged forgiveness for disobeying his uncle and taking part in the attack on Lawton's warehouse. It was entirely his own fault, he said, that he'd been seized by British soldiers and imprisoned at Fort William. Mrs. Gifford exclaimed with horror over Sally, dressed in boys' clothes *and* shaking uncontrollably. Mr. Gifford was outraged that Mr. Lawton had brought British soldiers into Boston. "We can't stand for that!"

Then Felicity Gifford declared, "What are we thinking, chattering on and on? It can wait until morning. Sally, Ethan: straight to bed."

Sally was eager to obey, but Ethan asked permission to go tell his parents he was home safe.

"What!" William Gifford sputtered. "Your folks don't know yet? You thoughtless young scamp!" Scowling, he shook a finger in front of Ethan's nose. "You deserve to get the strapping of your life." Turning to the door, he pulled on his cloak over his nightshirt. "Do as Mrs. Gifford says. I'll tell Frank and Patience."

A few minutes later, Sally was in bed with a hot brick wrapped in a towel at her feet. Even so, she couldn't stop shivering. Felicity Gifford brought her a steaming mug of herbal tea and watched while Sally sipped. Mrs. Gifford kept shaking her head and pressing a hand over her heart. "Fort *William*," she muttered. "Dressed as a *lad*. Haven't I brought you up right?"

Sally was sure she was in for weeks — perhaps months — of scolding for tonight's adventure. But she was too tired to worry about that now. As her eyelids sank shut, her stepmother took the empty mug from her hands and tucked the quilt around her more snugly.

When the sun was up and the family was awake again, William Gifford examined his nephew carefully, from his bruised face to his scraped shins. "It seems the British already gave you a good beating — I suppose *I* don't need to strap you." He looked relieved. Father hated giving punishment, thought Sally, even when it was deserved.

No one suggested that Sally should be punished, but when she returned from taking Josiah to Dame Hewes, her father and her stepmother were waiting for her in the kitchen. Felicity Gifford began: "Sarah, do you understand how wrong and foolish you were, going out in the town by yourself in the middle of the night?

"Yes, ma'am, it was wrong and foolish," Sally answered. "I'm sorry. I couldn't think of what else to do." She added quickly, "But I wasn't by myself."

Mr. Gifford drew his breath in sharply. "I was afraid of that. Of course, you couldn't have rescued Ethan from the fort on your own." He seemed angry and worried, although Sally wasn't sure why.

"Who *was* with you?" demanded Mrs. Gifford. "Was it Harry Cole talked you into such a wild scheme?"

"Harry!" exclaimed Sally. The thought of sneaking around in the dark with Harry Cole made her shiver. "No, ma'am. It was James." As her father and stepmother stared at her openmouthed, Sally went on, "James Lawton. It was his idea. He knew all about the fort. Except, he was wrong about the sentries."

"James Lawton? Edmund Lawton's son?" Sally's father looked as if he couldn't believe his ears. Sally nodded.

"James Lawton!" said Felicity Gifford. "Whoever would have thought?"

"Now I see how it was." Mr. Gifford spoke slowly, lifting his leather apron off its peg. "Mr. Lawton knew that Ethan was seized and taken to the fort. So James Lawton found out from his father. And James came to the shop yesterday to tell you."

"James was so afraid for his family," Sally explained. "He made me promise not to tell anyone."

Her stepmother gave her a severe look. "That was very wrong of you, not to tell your father and me. I thought I'd taught you better than that." In a milder tone she said to her husband, "Imagine: James went against his own father to help Ethan."

William Gifford shook his head in wonderment as he tied his apron strings. "Didn't I remark to you at the time, how odd it was — to be sure, James is an odd lad — that he pulled his heel off for an excuse to see the shoemaker?"

Mrs. Gifford raised an eyebrow at Sally. "Yes, and I thought Master Lawton must be sweet on the shoemaker's daughter."

Sally's face grew warm. James Lawton, "sweet" on her! What an embarrassing idea. She was thankful that her cousin was working in the shop already and couldn't tease her about this. She muttered, "James only wanted to help Ethan."

As for Ethan, he went about his duties soberly all day. Late in the afternoon, Sally peeked in the workshop and found him alone. She went up to the workbench. "Ethan . . . Was it very bad, in the guardhouse?"

Ethan glanced up at her. "Very bad? I hope to heaven I never land in such a place again." He was silent for a moment, looking down at the leather he was trimming, and Sally thought maybe he'd rather not talk about it.

"But the worst thing," he went on in a low voice, "was thinking about where they were sending me. The other prisoner in my cell kept telling me how they'd treat me in the British navy. How they'd make me eat wormy hard tack and do the crew's dirty work and sleep in the bilge water, and they'd flog me if I so much as looked an officer in the eye. He wouldn't shut up."

"Another prisoner told you that?" Sally was shocked.

"How could he?"

"I think he was trying to take his mind off what was going to happen to him," said Ethan heavily. "He'd been caught deserting for the second time."

Sally was silent. Besides imagining a short, nasty life in the British navy, Ethan had been locked up in the dark with a condemned man. No wonder he was quiet today.

"I was praying for rescue," her cousin went on, "but I thought no one knew where I was. I never dreamed — " Ethan suddenly looked into her eyes. "You're a brave girl, Sally Gifford. No one ever had a better cousin."

"No, you shouldn't say that!" Sally tore her gaze away. "It was my fault you got caught. I warned Kitty . . . I didn't think you'd go out with the gang . . . I didn't think . . ." She glanced at Ethan. To her amazement, he was grinning.

"I guessed as much," Ethan said. "You were looking out for your dear Miss Lawton, hmm? Still, it was my own fault for depending on Harry Cole." Ethan's smile faded. "He's not as clever — or as brave — as he lets on."

The next day, Sunday, Sally was glad for a day of rest. So were Mr. and Mrs. Gifford, evidently, because they both dozed off in church during the sermon.

That afternoon, Sally fetched the pen, ink, and paper to write to Hannah as usual and waited for her father to dictate his message. William Gifford muttered under his breath, stopped, shook his head, and muttered some more, as if he was having trouble finding the right words. "Say, Cousin

Ethan was in great danger — no. Say, your sister was foolhardy but very brave . . . no, better not say that." Finally Mr. Gifford threw up his hands. "Best not to set it down in writing at all. We'll tell Tom, and he can tell Hannah."

Felicity nodded. "Letters can fall into the wrong hands."

Sally winced. Of course Felicity didn't know about her letter to Kitty, read by Mr. Lawton, or Kitty's letter to Sally, read by Hannah, but it was still a painful memory to Sally.

"Tell Hannah" — Mr. Gifford chuckled — "tell her she'll have to pry the news out of Tom, if she can!" With Tom Greene as messenger, the problem was not that he'd tell too much, but that he'd leave out all the interesting details.

The next day was washday, and as usual Sally fetched water from the well to fill the copper boiler. Normally Sally didn't think twice about hauling bucket after heavy bucket, but today her arms still ached from Friday night's laborious rowing. She'd been so thankful when the unwieldy British boat had finally bumped against the dock in Boston. As soon as the three of them were off the boat, Ethan had given it a good shove into the harbor. "The tide will take it out for Admiral Montagu to find," he declared.

While Sally and Felicity Gifford went about their washday work, Baby Lucy was kept safe in a hamper with the lid off. The baby was nearly walking now, and they couldn't watch her every minute. "Don't fuss," Sally told Lucy, giving her little sister a wooden paddle to play with. Gathering clothes to be washed, Sally picked up Ethan's outgrown breeches from the floor where she'd dropped them. If she needed proof that she'd really been to Fort William and back, the breeches showed it. Green streaks on the knees marked where she'd knelt on the scummy dock, and the seat of the pants looked as if she'd sat on bird droppings. The stolen boat must have been splattered with them.

As Sally dropped the breeches into the copper laundry boiler, Mrs. Gifford gave her a stern look. "You knew I was saving those breeches for Josiah."

Sally nodded meekly.

"As well as the jacket." Stirring the simmering pot, Felicity nodded across the room at Sally's workbasket, with Ethan's outgrown jacket folded on top. "You have quite a rip to mend now. Luckily it's on the seam."

"Yes, ma'am," Sally answered her stepmother. How had the jacket torn? Maybe as she struggled toward the door of the guardhouse, towing Ethan. One of the prisoners had jostled her on the way out. She'd felt the jacket catch on something in the dark.

With another stern glance at Sally, Mrs. Gifford went on, "I can't approve of your wearing boys' clothes."

"No, ma'am." Sally realized how peculiar the neighbors would think her, to say nothing of Pastor Bacon at Old South Meeting House, if the word got around.

"But if you *were* bound and determined to go off on such a reckless, foolhardy jaunt . . . I suppose it was sensible to dress like a lad." Something like a smile quivered at the corners of Felicity Gifford's mouth.

16

A DREAM COME TRUE

In the following days, Kitty left increasingly anxious notes for Sally in the hollow tree.

> *Papa says the governor must call for Colonel Leslie's Troops to protect us. Now the skiff from Papa's Barge is missing — stolen. Meanwhile, Mrs. Knowlton has left our Household to join her brother in New York! She couldn't feel safe here, she said. How does she suppose I feel?*

Sally didn't answer. She felt mistrustful of Kitty. She remembered what Tom Greene had said: "You're friends with the Tory girl, you see? Accidents are bound to happen." Still, Sally couldn't help worrying about her.

Kitty's next note read:

Papa says the Governor's Council will not agree to ask for protection from Fort William. Papa says harsh things about the Governor's lack of Courage. Sally, we may have to leave Boston entirely! We must be ready at a Moment's notice — my Hatbox is packed. But Papa will not promise to take my Spinet.

Dear Friend, be prepared!

Sally puzzled over the last sentence. What should she be "prepared" for — to say farewell?

That night, as the Giffords were getting ready for bed, Sally heard an ominous noise outside, in the direction of Marlborough Street. It began as a sort of muttering and growling, then rose to a roar, accented with shouts and thuds. Sally looked at her father. William Gifford seemed to be listening to the noise, too, but he locked the shutters without commenting.

Lying in bed and listening, Sally wondered who the night watchman was tonight. What he was doing? He certainly wasn't blowing his horn to arouse the neighborhood and stop the riot.

The next morning, Sally found another note in the old apple tree. The paper was torn, as if Kitty had ripped a page from a book, and the script was marred with spatters of ink.

Marlborough Street,
27th November
Dear Sally,
The Mob attacked our house last night. They bellowed vile

Oaths. They heaved cobblestones through the windows and smashed my Spinet! We — James and I — must flee to the Governor's town residence for safety. They threatened to murder Papa! He leaves for Castle Island. These are terrible times. Only believe in me, dear Friend! I have a Plan, and Papa will — he must — agree. Be ready.

Everyone up and down Winter Street knew about the attack on the Lawtons' house, although no one had rushed to their defense last night. When Sally took Josiah to Dame Hewes' house, the old woman was discussing it with a neighbor. "I don't say the mob is right, but what can Mr. Lawton expect?"

Later that day Sally wrote Kitty an answer, begging her to explain her plan. But before she could take her letter to the hollow tree, Ethan popped into the kitchen with the news that the Lawtons had left their house. "They had piles of baggage strapped on the top of the carriage."

Just like that, Kitty had been whisked away to Governor Hutchinson's house in the North End. The North End was the other side of town, several miles away from Winter Street.

"Mr. Lawton saw me watching," Ethan added, "and he gave me a deadly look."

"No doubt he believes you were in the mob last night," said Felicity Gifford dryly.

Ethan flushed. "But I wasn't. I think it was cowardly, to attack a house with women and children in it."

Sally's mind was fixed on the gap widening between her

and Kitty. The North End! She couldn't imagine a single excuse she might give for going there. Now it would be almost impossible for the girls to exchange messages.

The first of the tea ships arrived in Boston Harbor on the very next day, a Sunday. It was the *Dartmouth*, owned by Francis Rotch. Men from the waterfront burst into Old South Meeting House with the news, interrupting Pastor Bacon's sermon. "The *Dartmouth's* anchored off of Long Wharf!" they shouted. It went without saying that the ship and its cargo of tea was now under the protection of the British admiral's flagship, the sixty-four gun HMS *Captain*.

On Monday, thousands of Boston citizens crammed into the Old South Meeting House — not for a church service, but to decide what to do about the tea. They voted to serve Mr. Rotch with a formal warning: If he attempted to unload the *Dartmouth's* cargo of tea, it would be at his "Peril." Town meeting ordered that the *Dartmouth* be moved to Griffin's wharf and guarded day and night by men loyal to the town.

For the next two weeks, it was a standoff between the tea agents, backed by Governor Hutchinson and the British navy, and the town of Boston. The tea agents wanted to unload the tea, sell it, and collect their profits. The town wanted to force the tea ships to turn around and sail back to Britain without unloading.

On December 3rd the second tea ship, the *Eleanor*, arrived in Boston and joined the *Dartmouth* at Griffin's Wharf, and the tension grew. The following week the third tea ship, the *Beaver*, sailed into Boston Harbor. There was smallpox as well as tea on the *Beaver*, so that ship had to be fumigated before it docked. The joke around town was that tea was a worse plague than the pox.

No one got much work done, and there was a great deal of standing around talking, in spite of the December cold. One afternoon, as Sally left to fetch Josiah home, Felicity Gifford was leaning on the backyard fence, talking with a neighbor. A single word kept popping out of their murmured conversation: "Tea . . . tea . . . tea . . ."

At Dame Hewes', Sally found the old woman on her doorstep, arguing with a firewood peddler. "If I was guarding the *Dartmouth*" — the peddler waved in the direction of the tea ships at Griffin's Wharf — "I'd take a torch to it. That'd put an end to all this nonsense."

"Not so fast! The tea agents may still resign," said Dame Hewes. "The tea agents in Philadelphia and New York gave in, so why should ours hold out?" She patted Josiah on the head absently as the boy came out of her house, tossing and catching his beanbag. Sally suspected the children hadn't made much progress in their primers today.

"But in Philadelphia and New York," the peddler answered Dame Hewes, "there isn't a Fort William guarding the harbor with its cannon, and there isn't an Admiral Montagu blocking the channels with his warships, eh? Besides, the tea agents can sit on Castle Island until doomsday." He laughed unpleasantly. "But they'd better make haste to move their families out there, too, or — "

"I should hope the Sons of Liberty aren't such savages as to attack women and children!" exclaimed Dame Hewes. Sally, hustling Josiah away from the peddler's hateful chuckle, wondered if Dame Hewes was right. Sally wouldn't trust Harry Cole, for example, to be so gallant. If Kitty and James were in danger, that was nothing to laugh about.

As Sally walked Josiah back home, he coaxed her into playing catch with him. The beanbag gentleman she'd sewed was badly faded, and loose embroidery threads fluttered as he flew back and forth.

While Sally helped prepare supper and kept Baby Lucy out from underfoot, she thought of Kitty and James, huddled in the governor's mansion. Were they safe? She pictured the mob howling down on them like a nor'easter, those violent storms that attacked Boston every winter. Mr. Samuel Adams had stirred up Harry Cole's boys and the other gangs, but could he keep them in line?

Still worrying about the Lawtons, Sally went to the workshop to call her father to supper. William Gifford sat at his workbench, but he was not working. He looked up from the letter in his hand.

Sally was alarmed. "What is it, Father?" He'd never looked at her like that, even on that dreadful night when Mr. Lawton came for the gold ring.

"Sarah Gifford," he said slowly. "Have you been planning this all along? Is this what you want, then?"

"What *is* it?"

For answer, he handed her the letter. Sally ran her eyes over the elegant script:

> *Castle Island,*
> *15th December.*
> *To William Gifford, Shoemaker:*
> *Regarding the present Disturbances in the Town, I find it ex-pedient to remove my Family to the shelter of Fort William, and in all likelihood to quit Massachusetts Colony altogether as soon as convenient. As you are aware, my Daughter is very fond of your Sarah, and it seems that her happiness in Exile would be assured if she had her company. Therefore, I propose to accept your girl into my Family. Even though it is possible that I will lose my hold-ings in Boston, you may be confident that she would have every Advantage that wealth and position can offer. My investments in the West Indies are considerable, and I am in possession of a well-appointed House in London.*
>
> *An immediate Answer is requested — indeed, your daughter will need to join my Family at the Governor's town residence this very afternoon, for they leave Boston in haste.*
>
> *I am, Sir, most sincerely yours,*
> *Edmund Lawton, Merchant*

Mr. Lawton's wordy phrases swam in Sally's head. Did he mean what the letter seemed to say? Had Kitty actually persuaded her father to adopt Sally? Sally felt as if she'd fall-en into a different world, the world of her own daydreams.

As Sally looked from Mr. Lawton's letter to her father's stricken face, Ethan burst into the shop. "They're calling for us to stand ready tomorrow," he announced. "Some of us apprentices. Uncle William, sir, will you let me go?" Ethan paused, glancing from Mr. Gifford to Sally and back again. "I wouldn't go out again without your permission . . ." His voice trailed off, and then he asked, "Are you well, Uncle?"

Sally longed to do something to take that grim look from her father's face. "Father, I didn't know . . ." she started. "It wasn't my idea . . ." But it was Sally's idea. She, Sally, had longed for just such an outlandish happening, straight from one of Kitty's novels. Now it had come true.

Ignoring Ethan, her father repeated, "Is this what you want? To become Sarah . . . *Lawton?*"

Grabbing the letter from Sally, Ethan scowled at the flowing handwriting. "Mr. Lawton! What's he trying to say? Why can't he say it straight out? — Oh." He looked at Sally. "'Every Advantage.' Pink flounced dresses and spinet lessons."

As Sally tried to find words to answer her father, Mr. Gifford spoke heavily. "I must talk this over with Mrs. Gifford. She's the one who would have to give up your help. I don't know how she could manage." He turned to Ethan, as if his nephew's request had just sunk in. "And you! Didn't you have enough of beatings and prison? What would your father say to me if I allowed you go with the mob again?"

"He would say, many thanks," Ethan assured him. "It's not the mob, and I won't go with Harry Cole's gang. Father's going, too."

Throwing up his hands, William Gifford pushed himself up from the bench. "The world is going mad — beginning with my own kin." He disappeared into the kitchen.

Sally felt as if she were standing with one foot on a dock and the other in a boat. The boat was slipping away from the dock, and every instant, the water between boat and dock widened. She had to leap one way or the other.

Ethan was gazing at her. He looked surprised and disappointed, but not shocked. Sally exclaimed, "Stop looking at me! You have no right." Without waiting for an answer, she dashed out the front door of the workshop, into the street.

Sally's head seemed to be full of wild music. She didn't know where she was going — only that she had to go off by herself. She ran across Common Street, into the Mall. A brisk wind blew across the fields and through the bare trees, and she had no shawl.

Sally's feet took her to the end of the Mall, into the Granary burying ground. She stopped at the granite slab that marked her mother's grave. "Mama," she began.

Then Sally paused. She was not a little child. She had braved a fort full of soldiers to rescue her cousin. She was too old to call her mother "Mama." Besides, Hannah might be right. Maybe Sarah Gifford would have been cross with Sally almost as often as Mother Felicity was.

"Mother," Sally began again. "My grandfather fought with the crew against the captain, because the captain was unjust. He lost his life, and you had to grow up poor, but you were proud of him." Sally took a deep breath, and her voice broke. "I'm proud of him, too, proud of my family: the Downses, the Giffords. My family."

17

DAUGHTER OF LIBERTY

Sally ran, then walked until she caught her breath, then ran again. Common Street led to Tremont Street, which led to Hanover Street, which ended at Mill Creek. Across the bridge over Mill Creek and, finally, into the North End. The afternoon was almost gone. Would she be too late?

Sally had seen Governor Hutchinson's mansion in the North End of Boston only once before, on the way to the Charlestown ferry. But she knew where it was: just past the Cockerel Church, with its brass rooster weathervane.

The governor's house was as large as a church itself, but fancier than most of the churches in Boston. Columns on each side of the front of the house, as well as two columns flanking the front door, ran all the way up to the top of the third story. A balcony hung over the front door.

Outside the fence a group of onlookers loitered. They

peered over the railing and pointed at people hurrying behind the rows of windows. The ironwork gate of the mansion stood open, and so did the front door. Servants bustled back and forth, carrying barrels and trunks and hampers to a wagon outside the gate.

The wagon blocked half the street, and drivers of carts and carriages edging past the wagon shouted insults.

"Good riddance to bad rubbish, Lawton!"

"Aye, get out of town now, or leave with a coat of tar and feathers!"

However, Mr. Lawton was nowhere to be seen. The servants ignored the taunts, except to take a swipe or two at bystanders who crowded too close.

Ducking around the workers, Sally hurried up the walk and into the front hall of the governor's mansion. A many-armed brass chandelier hung overhead, and the floor was polished wood parquet. The elegant space seemed made for gentlemen and ladies to stroll through it to the grand staircase. But today the chandelier was dark, and the floor was cluttered with trunks, bundles, and a jumble of loose items. Sally recognized the ivory-colored globe, on its mahogany stand, from the Lawtons' library.

On top of a dressing table, a portrait leaned against the wall. A portrait of a girl in a plain gray dress? No — that wasn't a picture, but a scroll-framed looking glass, the one from Kitty's bedroom. The girl was Sally.

Beyond the dressing table, James knelt in front of an open trunk full of books. He muttered to himself, "I must have Newton's *Optics*." He removed one book from the trunk and replaced it with another from a pile of books on the floor. Then he looked at the book in his hand, stroking its spine. "But I can't leave *Systema Naturae*."

One of the servants paused beside him. "Master James, there's no time for that! The wagon leaves in a quarter-hour." James groaned.

"James?" said Sally.

He raised his head and focused a puzzled stare on her. "What are you doing here?"

"I came to — " Sally's throat tightened. "Where's Kitty?"

He shrugged and shook his head. Sally had never seen him so distracted, even on the day he'd been burned with tar.

While she was wondering where to look for Kitty, in this house with so many rooms, Kitty's own voice rang out. "Sally!" Sally looked up to see her friend poised on the landing of the staircase.

Kitty flew down the stairs, her face lit with joy. "Oh, Sally! I was afraid your father wouldn't let you come, and I waited and waited, and then I looked out the window one more time, and there you were at the gate! I should have trusted you." She pushed her way through the clutter and seized Sally's hands. "Where's your baggage? Did you give it to the porters?"

Sally looked into Kitty's shining eyes and then looked away. She felt heavy with sadness, weighed down as if there were a stone in her chest. "I didn't bring anything."

"Never mind, then," said Kitty. "You can borrow my things until we have a set of clothes made for you."

Sally didn't know what to say. This was harder than she'd expected.

As Sally hesitated, the joy faded from Kitty's face. "Is something wrong? What is it?"

Sally had to force the words from her mouth: "I came . . . to say goodbye."

Kitty looked down at her hands, still grasping Sally's. She let go. "Goodbye?" Her mouth trembled, and she touched the gold ring on her right hand. "They made us give back the tokens of our pledge, but I thought we were still sisters at heart."

"Oh, Kitty, you are still in my heart!" Sally's throat hurt as she talked. "And I'll never forget you. But I can't go with you. I belong with my own family."

Kitty gave an astonished laugh. "Your *family*? The Wicked Stepmother and the Loutish Apprentice and the Little Grub? You want to spend your days digging turnips and scrubbing soiled linen for them?"

Sally flushed, ashamed that she'd ever talked that way about Mother Felicity and Ethan and Josiah. She searched for the right words to explain to Kitty what she felt now. "It *was* lovely, playing music with you and acting plays and going out in fine clothes. I am so grateful for all that. And I know you must have had to plead and badger and pester your father until he agreed . . ."

"Yes, I did," said Kitty. "He vowed that no father ever

had such a tiresome daughter. Even so, he only gave in because he was so bedeviled with the tar and the mobs, and whether the tea will ever clear customs."

"But I can't go with you. I'm not your sister." Sally's voice broke, and she tried to clear her throat. "I'm Sally Gifford."

Kitty's eyes filled with tears, and Sally felt tears sting her own eyes in response. Once more she seemed very close to Kitty, as close as the two girls had been on the golden summer afternoons in the Lawtons' parlor.

Then Kitty blinked fiercely and lifted her chin. "Indeed? Well, *Sally Gifford*, it's kind of you to call on me, but you can see that I'm very busy here. I need to make sure the music for my spinet is packed." Kitty became angrier as she talked. "Of course the spinet itself was smashed by your fine *family* and friends, but Papa will buy me a new one, once we are settled in London."

"Ethan wasn't in that mob," Sally protested, but she knew that wasn't the point. Tears ran down her face as she moved toward the door, followed by Kitty's spiteful chatter. With blurred vision Sally glanced again at the looking-glass on the dressing table, the glass where she'd once seen herself as a young lady in a pink dress.

"Farewell, farewell," called Kitty from the stairs, as if Sally were a distant acquaintance. "Perhaps I'll think of you when I go to my first ball." She trilled a laugh. "Perhaps not."

James's trunk of books was closed now, and he was

lifting the globe off its stand. "This should be packed in a separate barrel," he told a servant, "and well padded with straw." The servant threw up his hands and rolled his eyes, but he went off to look for padding.

Sally paused in front of James, placing her fingertips on the ivory-colored globe. There was tiny Massachusetts, on one edge of the vast ocean, and tiny England on the opposite edge. She felt a further pang. It wasn't only Kitty that she was giving up. "Goodbye, James."

"Goodbye, Sally." Looking down at the globe, James spoke in a voice so low she could hardly hear him. "I wish you would come with us."

"I can't," she said. She hesitated. "I think you're very clever and brave and honorable."

Smiling wistfully, he made an awkward bow over the globe in his arms. "I think — er — likewise."

Sally smiled back and curtsied. She started to say goodbye once more, but her voice would not come out of her choked throat. She turned and hurried through the doorway.

On the front steps of the mansion, Sally wiped tears from her face with the back of her hand. She walked down the brick path to the gate. The December sun hung low over the Mill Cove, gleaming feebly on the Cockerel Church's weathervane. Sally would have to hurry, to get home in time to milk the cow.

Sally ran all the way home, but by the time she pounded down the alley, Ethan was crossing the backyard to the cowshed. He paused, fixing his gaze on her face. "Well? Is it Sally

Gifford or Sally Lawton?"

Sally was just able to gasp out one word at a time: "It's — Sally — Gifford!"

Ethan gave her a slow smile. With a gallant gesture, he held the cowshed door open for her.

A cold rain was falling the next morning as William Gifford left his shop for town meeting. Ethan went with him — he was too young to vote, but he could hang around the back of the hall and listen.

Today, December 16th, was the last day the *Dartmouth* could sit in the harbor without unloading its cargo of tea. By law, once a ship arrived in port it must unload and pay the customs duties within twenty days, or be seized by customs officials and sold at auction. If the tea was unloaded, it would certainly be sold, and that would end Boston's resistance to the Tea Act.

"What if the meeting decided to block the customs officials from boarding the ship tomorrow?" Sally asked her stepmother.

Mrs. Gifford looked grim, and she picked up Lucy and held her tight, as if to protect her. "That would be openly breaking the law. Then Colonel Leslie would have the right to send his soldiers into Boston. Or Admiral Montagu to fire on the town."

Sally was so on edge that she could hardly keep her mind on her chores. "Pay heed to what you're doing," Felicity Gifford told her. "You dressed Lucy with her smock inside out."

"Yes, ma'am," said Sally, pulling off the baby's smock. "Do I smell the bread burning?" Mrs. Gifford wasn't paying much heed to her work, either.

When Mr. Gifford and Ethan returned from town meeting for the midday meal, Tom Greene was with them. The men hung up their rain-sodden cloaks, and Sally handed them towels to dry off. "Tom, you came all the way from Concord?" she said in surprise. "You don't even come for market day, this time of year."

"Pleasant weather for a trip to town," said Tom with a straight face.

"You should have seen Tom's horse!" Ethan put in. "Mud up to his hocks."

"Tom wasn't the only man from the countryside at the meeting," said Mr. Gifford.

The smell of damp wool mingled with the steam from the chowder as the family sat down. Between spoonfuls, William Gifford told how the town meeting had voted. They'd decided to make the *Dartmouth's* owner, Francis Rotch, ask Governor Hutchinson to give the tea ships permits to carry their cargo back out of Boston Harbor. Then they could safely pass Admiral Montagu's fleet and the guns of Fort William.

"Poor Mr. Rotch," said Mr. Gifford with a little smile. "He has to slog all the way out to Milton to see the governor."

Ethan grinned at Tom. "Not as far as Mr. Greene slogged from Concord, but then Tom Greene was more willing."

"And it sounds like a fool's errand for Mr. Rotch, besides," put in Felicity Gifford. "Surely the governor will refuse?"

"I believe there's a plan, in that case." Mr. Gifford spoke calmly, but Ethan's eyes shone. Sally thought he looked as if he could hardly wait.

Late that afternoon, as Sally was lighting the candles in the kitchen, Ethan returned from Old South Meeting House. He was panting as if he'd run all the way. "The meeting is resolved," he gasped. "The meeting is resolved that — that the tea shall not be landed!"

"Did the governor refuse, then?" asked Sally.

"Mr. Rotch hasn't come back from Milton yet, but everyone knows the governor will refuse." Ethan caught his breath. "I have to be ready. They said to disguise ourselves. Sally, help me."

Disguise. Sally caught her breath as she realized what that meant. Ethan and Uncle Frank, along with many more, had decided to break the law. They needed to disguise themselves because if they were recognized, they could be arrested and punished.

Felicity spoke up from the fireplace, where she was stirring the stew. "Sally, over here. Here's soot for his face."

Sally rubbed her fingers over the blackened stones of the fireplace and smeared the soot on Ethan's forehead, nose, cheeks, and chin. His eyes and lips stood out, ghastly pale.

"How do I look?" asked Ethan.

"You look like a devil," Sally said sincerely. Josiah was

tugging at her sleeve, begging to be "dis-crised" like Ethan, so Sally dabbed some soot on his round cheeks.

Felicity pulled an old blanket out of the chest. "If even Frank Downs is joining this wild party tonight, I suppose they know what they're doing," she muttered.

Just as Felicity Gifford was draping the blanket around Ethan's shoulders, there was a sharp whistle outside the kitchen door. "That's the signal!" he exclaimed, picking up an axe.

"Be careful," said Felicity. "The rain stopped, thank heaven."

Ethan was headed out the door, singing, "In Freedom we're born and in Freedom we'll live!"

"Good luck," Sally called to him. *Did* the tea raiders know what they were doing? How could they be sure that the British warships wouldn't open fire on them? Or that Colonel Leslie wouldn't decide to send troops across the harbor to protect the tea?

A few minutes later, William Gifford appeared. "Has Ethan left?" Then he caught sight of Josiah's sooty face, and he laughed in surprise.

"Father, Sally dis-crised me and Ethan!" said the little boy.

"Did she?" William Gifford stooped to hold his son by the shoulders. "It's a game to you, isn't it?" His tone was fond, but sad. "I think we'll be playing the game long after this night, and in hard times ahead."

"I don't see what else we could do," said Felicity Gifford.

"No," said Mr. Gifford.

There was a pause, and then Felicity said, "I've been thinking: Perhaps now you'd want to give back — " She nodded toward Sally.

Sally's thoughts were following Ethan down to the harbor, and she didn't understand what Felicity Gifford was talking about. But her father nodded as if *he* understood. "Yes." He went into the workshop and returned with something in his hand. He stopped in front of Sally.

"Sarah Gifford," said her father. "You have earned the right to wear this brooch that your brave Grandfather Downs gave his beloved daughter, Sarah."

Sally caught her breath. She'd given up hope of ever seeing her treasure again.

Carefully William Gifford pinned the heart-shaped mother-of-pearl brooch on Sally's scarf. "My daughter. My daughter of liberty."

AUTHOR'S NOTE

Friends of Liberty ends on the night of Thursday, December 16, 1773, shortly before about a hundred men and boys boarded the three tea ships at Griffin's Wharf. They smashed open the chests of tea and dumped more than 90,000 pounds of tea leaves into Boston Harbor. It was hard, exciting work, and the only light was their torches and lanterns, but they were careful not to damage anything other than the tea.

Because the craftsmen, fishermen, apprentices, and merchants who joined in the Tea Party were breaking the law, they all swore not to tell who they were. And they didn't, until long afterward. By that time the United States of America had been an independent country for fifty years, so there was no risk that they would be punished. On the other hand, their memories weren't as reliable as they would have been earlier.

Even today, it's hard to know for sure who took part in the tea-dumping, but it certainly included all types of towns-folk. The silversmith Paul Revere was one of the raiders; another was a poor shoemaker named George Robert Twelves Hewes. John Hancock, the richest man in Boston, was probably not on board the tea ships that night, although many of the men in his militia were. Peter Slater, thirteen-year-old apprentice to a rope-maker, was locked up by his master, but he managed to sneak out and join the tea-dumpers. There were also fishermen (handy at unloading boats) like Sally's Uncle Frank among the raiders.

Whoever raided the tea ships that night, the Boston Tea Party spurred the American colonies toward open rebellion against the British Empire. Parliament reacted to the destruction of the tea by closing the port of Boston, taking away several rights written into the Massachusetts Charter, and sending General Thomas Gage with four regiments to occupy Boston again. The Massachusetts House of Representatives reacted to Parliament's repressive measures by voting to buy gunpowder. In 1774, the American colonies convened the First Continental Congress in Philadelphia. And in April 1775, with the battles of Lexington and Concord, the Revolutionary War began.

Sally hardly recognized her own face in the looking glass above Kitty's dressing table. At home, there was only one small hand mirror, spotted and dim, that Felicity Gifford used to see if the part in her hair was straight. In Kitty's scroll-framed looking glass, wearing Kitty's pink flounced dress, Sally looked like a portrait of a young lady.

Sally felt a thrill. Today, she could be a different person . . .

It's 1773, and Boston is in political turmoil. As tension rises between England and the colonies, lines are drawn between the Loyalists and the Patriots. And Sally Gifford, a shoemaker's daughter, finds herself on the opposite side from her best friend Kitty Lawton, the daughter of a wealthy merchant.

Sally is torn between her cherished friendship and her loyalties to her own family and community in their fight for freedom. As the conflict continues to grow more charged in the weeks leading up to the Boston Tea Party, Sally must decide exactly what is most important to her.

BEATRICE GORMLEY (www.beatricegormley.com) is the author of a number of award-winning children's books, including *Miriam* and *Maria Mitchell: The Soul of an Astronomer* (both Eerdmans), as well as *Salome* (Knopf). She lives in Massachusetts.

Cover illustration © 2013 Stephanie Dalton Cowan

EERDMANS BOOKS
for Young Readers
Grand Rapids/Cambridge
An imprint of Wm. B. Eerdmans Publishing Co.
www.eerdmans.com/youngreaders

ISBN 978-0-8028-5418-6